Laura Martin writes historical romances with an adventurous undercurrent. When not writing she spends her time working as a doctor in Cambridgeshire, where she lives with her husband. In her spare moments Laura loves to lose herself in a book, and has been known to read from cover to cover in a single day when the story is particularly gripping. She also loves to travel—especially to visit historical sites and far-flung shores.

Also by Laura Martin

The Housekeeper's Forbidden Earl
Her Secret Past with the Viscount
A Housemaid to Redeem Him
The Kiss That Made Her Countess

The Ashburton Reunion miniseries

Flirting with His Forbidden Lady
Falling for His Practical Wife

Matchmade Marriages miniseries

The Marquess Meets His Match
A Pretend Match for the Viscount
A Match to Fool Society

The Cinderella Shepherd Sisters miniseries

One Waltz with the Viscount
One Forbidden Kiss with the Laird

Discover more at millsandboon.co.uk.

A SECRET TO SHOCK THE EARL

Laura Martin

MILLS & BOON

All rights reserved including the right of reproduction in whole or in part in any form. This edition is published by arrangement with Harlequin Enterprises ULC.

This is a work of fiction. Names, characters, places, locations and incidents are purely fictional and bear no relationship to any real life individuals, living or dead, or to any actual places, business establishments, locations, events or incidents. Any resemblance is entirely coincidental.

Without limiting the exclusive rights of any author, contributor or the publisher of this publication, any unauthorised use of this publication to train generative artificial intelligence (AI) technologies is expressly prohibited. HarperCollins also exercise their rights under Article 4(3) of the Digital Single Market Directive 2019/790 and expressly reserve this publication from the text and data mining exception.

® and TM are trademarks owned and used by the trademark owner and/or its licensee. Trademarks marked with ® are registered with the United Kingdom Patent Office and/or the Office for Harmonisation in the Internal Market and in other countries.

First published in Great Britain 2026 by Mills & Boon, an imprint of HarperCollins*Publishers* Ltd, 1 London Bridge Street, London, SE1 9GF

www.harpercollins.co.uk

HarperCollins*Publishers*, Macken House, 39/40 Mayor Street Upper, Dublin 1, D01 C9W8, Ireland

A Secret to Shock the Earl © 2026 Laura Martin

ISBN: 978-0-263-41869-9

02/26

Printed and Bound in the UK using 100% Renewable Electricity at CPI Group (UK) Ltd, Croydon, CR0 4YY

For all the incredible nurses I've had the privilege to work with over the last fifteen years.

Prologue

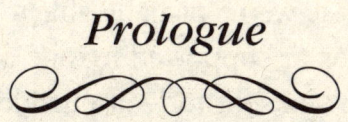

Portugal 1813

There were bodies everywhere. Men crying out in pain, calling out for mercy. Hands reached up and grabbed Hetty's skirt, trying to attract her attention. Now was the time to prove herself, to show the surgeons how indispensable she was.

'Primary assessment,' the doctor shouted, throwing a ball of ribbon her way.

Hetty Fairweather swallowed hard. This was the worst job, worse even than holding a man down whilst he had a limb amputated. Here she had to decide who would live and who would die, who was worth saving.

Putting all other thoughts from her mind, she fought her way through to the end of the makeshift ward and began with the first man. Her job was simple. She had to inspect each man's injuries and then decide if he should be boosted up the queue for treatment. There were three categories. The first were those with minor injuries, perhaps with cuts that needed sewing or superficial wounds that needed cleaning. These were normally able to walk, either by themselves or supported by one of their comrades. These she sent to wait outside in the little courtyard. Their wounds would be seen to, but not until those more seriously injured had been dealt with. Then there were the men with traumatic injuries, penetrating wounds to their limbs, gashes across their torsos, head injuries that rendered them confused or dazed. These were the men who might bleed out if they did not get swift medical attention. For these men she would cut a strip of ribbon and tie it around their wrist, signalling to the doctor to concentrate his efforts on the ones who were injured but could be saved.

The last group were the hardest to look in the eye. Men who had great gaping wounds to the abdomen or crush injuries to their legs from horses falling on them in battle. These men were likely to die no matter what was done for them. After she had passed up the line of soldiers, tying ribbons and making decisions, some orderlies would follow, lifting those who were too badly injured to move onto little truckle beds, covering them over and then leaving them to their groans of pain. If they were lucky, she would reach them with a drop of laudanum in time to ease their suffering and send them into a drowsy slumber.

Hetty was almost all the way up the line, approaching the altar of the church they had been given the use of as the field hospital whilst they were in Cidade Velha do Douro, when she saw a man in the uniform of a colonel. He was sitting quietly, not making any fuss despite the mangled mess of his left leg, his trousers soaked with blood. His eyes came up to meet hers and they were the bluest she had ever seen, a vibrant flash of colour amongst the drab browns and greys.

'May I look at your leg, sir?' she said, crouching down beside him. 'Do you know what happened?'

'A sword.' He shrugged. 'I think it went clean through.' He gave a little smile. 'I would wager none of the major vessels have been nicked, otherwise I would have been dead on the field.'

Hetty cut away the material of his trousers, inhaling sharply at the sight of the jagged wound on his thigh. It did indeed look as if a sword had run him through completely, piercing the muscles at front and back and only missing the bone and the major arteries by chance.

'You are a lucky man, Colonel.'

'A lucky man...or an unlucky one, depending on

your perspective. And perspective is important.' He winced as he shifted a little, no doubt uncomfortable from sitting on the cold, hard flagstones but unable to move properly because of his leg.

Hetty cut off some of the ribbon and took the Colonel's wrist, tying the fabric around it.

'I can give you something for the pain,' she said, seeing him grimace again.

'No,' he said sharply. 'I do not want anything that will addle my brain.'

'Sometimes an addled brain can be a blessing.' She thought of the brutal manner in which limbs were amputated. Any sensible man would take what she was offering.

'I will not lose my leg, miss, and I expect the surgeon will take one look at this mess and reach for his saw. I need to have my wits about me to stop him.'

'The surgery may save your life.'

'I can recover without it,' he said, giving her a wry half-smile. 'I'm a determined man.'

'Some problems determination cannot solve.'

She glanced up the line of soldiers. Her time was precious and she needed to get on, but something made her want to stay with this man. His quiet resolve, his humour despite his devastating injury. She would have liked to help him to a quieter part of the church, somewhere he could rest whilst she cleaned his wound, but she could not pick favourites. His rank as a colonel meant he would be seen by the surgeon quickly, but if he refused the treatment recommended, he would have to wait with the rest of the men.

With a last squeeze of his hand Hetty moved on, wondering if this man would still be alive when she returned.

Richard had never felt pain like it. This was far from his first injury but it was undoubtably the worst. He'd been shot almost a year earlier, the bullet lodging under his skin in the muscle just under his shoulder blade. Even when the surgeon had dug around with his forceps to pluck it out it had not hurt as much as this.

'You persuaded the surgeon not to amputate then?' Mrs Fairweather said. He had been pleased to see her friendly face as she bustled over with water and bandages, but now it was all he could do to stop himself from screaming at her. She was gentle but thorough, which he knew he should appreciate, but right now he wished she would stop cleaning and start bandaging.

'He told me I was a fool and that the wound would fester and I would be dead within the week. He also told me I was selfish to take a bed from a man who had a chance of recovery.'

'You stand by your decision?'

Richard grinned. 'I like your choice of words.'

Mrs Fairweather blushed and he found he could not tear his eyes from her face. She was pretty, even with her hair scraped back into a severe bun and her complexion pale from the long hours she had worked tirelessly today. There was kindness in her eyes and in the way she paused when he spoke to her, listening intently to what he said.

'This is going to hurt,' she said as she lifted his leg, showing remarkable strength as she held it in one hand whilst she tucked the first part of the bandage underneath.

Richard closed his eyes and thought of his beloved Northumberland. He could almost taste the salt in the air along the clifftops and feel the grass beneath his feet. It had been a long time since he had walked on Northumberland soil and perhaps once he had recovered and the battle for the Peninsular won, he would request leave to return home. Farnleigh Hall was his eldest brother's residence now. George had inherited the title on the death of their father three years earlier. Richard shared a close bond with all three of his elder brothers, but as the youngest he had felt the need to go out and prove himself, to make his own way in the world. Now a colonel in the army, he had achieved what he had set out to do, but perhaps a few weeks riding through the Northumberland countryside and sharing a drink with his brothers would be just what he needed.

'There,' Mrs Fairweather said, inspecting her work with an air of satisfaction.

'You were so gentle I barely felt a thing.'

'Flattery will serve you well, Colonel. I will see if there is an extra pillow for you to rest your leg upon.'

'Thank you.'

He watched as she disappeared amongst the rows of soldiers. Only his rank had saved him from being sent to the curtained-off area at the back of the church where they put those who were unlikely to survive. He had caught a glimpse of the rows of men, slumped over, faces ashen, calling out and groaning or even worse, deathly silent. Not for the first time, he wondered if his obstinance would cost him his life, but he refused to believe he could not survive this injury *and* keep his leg.

Hetty looked down at the Colonel's face and felt a ripple of unease. It was three days since the battle, three days since the influx of soldiers, and over half of those injured had now been quietly buried behind the church. Their wounds had been too deep, their injuries too severe, the medical care they'd received too basic.

She shouldn't have favourites, but out of everyone Hetty hoped the Colonel would survive. He was stoical despite the huge amount of pain he must be in, and never barked an order at her or showed any impatience as she worked her way up the line of patients, attending to their dressings or helping them with their meals. For three days she had changed his bandages and washed his wound, watching the flesh become stretched and red, radiating heat. The surgeon had visited again, a courtesy because of the Colonel's rank, but still the man had refused amputation.

Now it was three o'clock in the morning. Hetty had been unable to sleep. She had a basic little room with a bed and a basin for washing in on the upper floor of a local family's home. They were welcoming and kind and invited her to share their meals, but Hetty found it difficult to sleep in the hot little room at the top of the rickety stairs. Often, she would rise well before dawn and slip into the church they were using as a hospital. She would check on her patients and then sit in the cool darkness, enjoying the peace before a busy day.

Tonight though, she had found the Colonel thrashing about, his brow drenched in sweat and his skin hot to touch.

Immediately she'd gone to work, fetching a bucket of water from the well in the courtyard and using it to try and cool him. His wound had festered, as the doctors had predicted, and infection was now taking over his body. When there was more light she would peel back the bandages and see how bad things were underneath, but for now all she could do was keep him cool and comfortable.

As the sun began filtering in through the church windows Hetty heard the footsteps of the surgeon as he arrived for another day. There were rumours of a further offensive in the coming days, which would mean another round of casualties, another tense day spent amputating limbs and suturing wounds. It was a necessary job, but one she often wished she could leave behind.

Yet she was trapped here, with no funds to pay for a passage home and no family to send her any form of help. She had been totally reliant on her husband and when he had disappeared in battle six months earlier, she had realised how fragile and unstable her whole world was. He'd left her nothing—no money and no way to get home after insisting she follow the army so far across Europe for his comfort. These last six months she had made herself useful, working as a nurse, assisting the surgeons who worked alongside the battlefield. She had no training, no former knowledge, but she did possess a sensible attitude and was not squeamish. In the time she had been working she had quickly picked up the skills she needed and now was confident in her abilities. In return, she had a job that paid enough for her lodgings and meals, and very slowly she was saving any excess to pay for the journey home.

'The Colonel has succumbed, I see,' Mr Mortimer said, eyeing the man's flushed face from the end of the bed.

'He has a strong constitution and a stronger will,' Hetty replied quietly. 'He may surprise us yet.'

She had great respect for Mr Mortimer. The surgeon was skilled and worked tirelessly, but sometimes she wondered if the compassion had been beaten out of him by the relentless parade of horrifically wounded soldiers.

Mr Mortimer softened a little at the defiant note in Hetty's voice. 'Let us hope so. I am sure there are people back home eagerly awaiting his return. Finish up here, Mrs Fairweather, and then please ensure the operating room is ready. I fear we will be busy today.'

Before she left the Colonel, Hetty changed the bandages on his leg, grimacing as she saw the wound underneath. In all likelihood, this man would die in the next few days, losing his fight against the putrefaction of his wound. The idea made a lump form in Hetty's throat and she had to blink away the tears before she could apply a new bandage.

Richard leaned in a little closer to the candle. It was made of tallow, cheap and inefficient, and for a moment he felt ridiculous wishing for the pure beeswax candles they used at Farnleigh Hall. There were many more obvious home comforts to miss, such as a proper bed or a feather pillow or food fit for human consumption, yet it was the bright light of a wax candle he yearned for now.

'You're awake,' Hetty said as she slipped in, lowering the makeshift curtain that gave him a little privacy from the other men. She was carrying a little bundle of bread and cheese and as she unwrapped it Richard pushed himself further up in bed. 'And looking well.'

'I have persuaded the surgeon that I am not going to die, although he still seems eager to take my leg.'

'His whole purpose is amputation, Richard,' Hetty said as she broke the bread in half and handed him a chunk alongside a generous portion of cheese. Normally he was a stickler for the rules of Society, but at some point in the haze of the last two weeks he and

Hetty had progressed to using first names. She was a widow, a respectable woman, and if anyone else was in earshot he would call her Mrs Fairweather, but when it was just the two of them he felt an illicit thrill every time her name passed his lips.

Somewhere deep inside, Richard knew he was in love. He'd never been in love before, but the obsession he felt was unmistakable. Every moment he did not see her he was thinking about her. They had spent hours talking, late into the night. She had told him of her husband's disappearance, how it had left her stranded here in Portugal with no way of getting home. She had told him of the work she had been doing, of the satisfaction she felt at turning her hand to something useful, something more fulfilling than the domestic drudgery she had spent the few years of married life trudging through. They had spoken of her childhood, of her need to escape a father who became violent when drunk, with the consequence that she'd married the first half-suitable man who'd shown an interest.

In return, he had told her about Northumberland, his love of the land and the people, and the realisation that he did not have a true place there. As the youngest of four brothers, he was neither the heir nor the spare, and although his family were close and his brothers would always support him, he'd had a strong sense of wanting to make his own way in the world.

'Did you ever imagine a life like this for yourself?' Richard asked, gesturing vaguely at their surroundings.

Hetty laughed, stifling the sound with her hand. This was another thing he found irresistible about her. Her life had not followed the path she had expected, but she had adapted, bent with the change rather than allowing it to break her, and now she could find humour in the situation.

'No, but I am thankful in so many ways. I like helping people, and if I had stayed in my sleepy village in Essex I would never have had the chance to work alongside surgeons such as Mr Mortimer.'

'What will you do when you return home?'

She cocked her head to the side and thought about this carefully. Richard knew she was saving for the return passage by boat to England, slowly but steadily, and that she should have enough funds in a couple of months.

'I don't wish to be assistant to a surgeon, but I do wish to help people. I get great satisfaction from my work, but I would be happy if I never saw another amputation or abdominal wound again.'

'A nurse then, for injured soldiers who make it back home?'

'I think something like that would be ideal.' She shrugged. 'If I am honest, I cannot think past the next few days.'

Richard grimaced. He knew exactly what she meant. He had saved his leg and beaten the fever that had threatened his life, but as yet there was still a long road to recovery before he was fit to get back up on his horse and take command of his men. His immediate destination once he was recovered was clear—there was no way he would abandon his comrades in the middle of the war, but once the battle for the Peninsular was won, perhaps it was time to seek another path in life away from the violence.

He wondered if it was a remnant of the delirium he had experienced to be considering asking Hetty to marry him. They had known each other only a few weeks and for much of that he had been slipping in and out of consciousness, yet Richard felt with a certainty that he hadn't experienced before that he was destined to spend his life with this woman.

Hetty might not be able to think past the next few days, but as he had lain in bed recovering he'd had little else to occupy his time. Theirs would not be a scandalous match. Hetty was from a respectable family from the gentry class. She might not have the title or wealth of the women his elder brothers would be expected to marry, but as the fourth son he had a little more freedom. He thought he and Hetty could be quite happy with a modest house somewhere in Northumberland, perhaps with a view of the sea.

'I brought you another gift,' Hetty said, her eyes lighting up. She stood and hurried off, reappearing a minute later with two long wooden crutches. 'I thought you might like to get back on your feet again, start building the strength in your leg.'

'There is nothing I want more,' he said. Yesterday he'd tried to stand, managing to haul himself up but having to hop across the gap between the bed and the wall. His leg was still too sore to put much weight on yet, but with the help of crutches he would gradually regain use of it.

'Would you like me to help you now?'

Richard levered himself to the edge of the bed, using the strength in his arms to push himself up and then slotting the crutches so the upper bar rested in his armpits. It was an odd sensation, but after a few hopping steps around the little room he got the hang of the movement and found he could get about quite well. Hetty was right there beside him, one hand on his lower back, the other ready to catch him if he fell.

'You're a natural,' she said with a smile.

'It feels good to be up and about. I feared I would never leave that bed again.'

'I think you will recover just fine. Perhaps you

will be left with a limp…but I expect you could make even that seem distinguished.'

He turned to her, glad to be on a more equal footing now he was standing, rather than her sitting next to him whilst he was propped up in bed.

'I do not think I would have survived these last few weeks had it not been for your care, Hetty.'

'It is my job.'

He shook his head. 'Your job is to suture and clean and bandage our wounds. You have done so much more for me than that. Even when I was caught in the worst of the fever, I felt your presence tethering me to this earth, ensuring I had the best chance of surviving.'

She bit her lip, an unconscious move that made his eyes flick down to the rosy pink of her mouth, and in that instant he knew he had to kiss her. Ever so slowly he leaned in, feeling her eyes on him, her breath becoming heavier as she realised what was about to happen.

The kiss was sweet and sensual and everything he had dreamed of the last few weeks. He reached up and caressed her neck, relishing the feel of the soft skin beneath his fingertips.

'I know we shouldn't…' Hetty said as they pulled apart and then she smiled softly, raised herself up and brushed her lips against his.

The constant stress of battle, the threat of injury and death, had changed how Richard saw the world, and he expected it was the same for Hetty. Never in England would he contemplate kissing a woman he had only known a few short weeks, but here in Portugal, with the risk of Napoleon's forces attacking at any time, priorities were different.

'Whatever happens, Hetty, I will be there for you,' Richard said, looking deep into her eyes. 'I give you my vow.'

Richard paced across the courtyard of the church that was being used as a hospital, rehearsing the words in his head, wanting everything to be perfect. The last couple of days he had thought of nothing but this moment, and now it was here he was eager to let Hetty know what was in his heart.

He glanced again at the heavy wooden doors, knowing she would come out as soon as she could. Currently, Hetty was assisting Mr Mortimer in a particularly difficult amputation. The patient had stopped screaming a few minutes earlier, no doubt passed out from the pain and the horror of what was happening to him. From his time at the field hospital, Richard knew the surgeon would be working quickly now, trying to complete the operation before the patient woke up.

He grimaced, aware this was not the most romantic setting for what he was about to do, but they were in the middle of a war and orders would come through any day for his regiment to mount and leave the peaceful little village of Cidade Velha do Douro. Hetty would follow the army, but not necessarily his regiment, who travelled more swiftly on horseback than the foot soldiers could. They would be separated, perhaps for months, and before that happened, he wanted to make sure that once the fighting was over Hetty would come back to him.

Taking the plain metal band from his pocket, he held it up so it caught the sun. It was not a ring he would dare to propose with in ordinary times, but these were anything but normal. He had asked the blacksmith who travelled with their regiment to make something that would suffice until he could buy Hetty a prettier ring, and the blacksmith had been happy to oblige, pleased to turn his hand to something other than horseshoes.

As he replaced the ring in his pocket, he saw a flash of blue and then caught sight of Major Redfern, his second-in-command, running towards him as if chased by the devil himself.

'Attack!' Redfern bellowed. 'The French are attacking the village from the east.' He grabbed Richard by the arm and together they began racing towards the stables. Richard cast a glance over his shoulder. His instinct was to protect Hetty, but the best chance they had at defending the whole village, including the woman he loved, was for him to mount and take command of his men. Together they would be able to drive out the enemy soldiers. Hetty should be safe in the church—they would be able to cut off the French soldiers long before they got to that part of the village.

Despite the years of enforced physical exertion in the army he was panting by the time he reached the stables, but he did not lose a second between arriving and vaulting up onto his horse. It was chaos, with men everywhere, rushing in from all directions, but once they saw Richard on horseback, order quickly followed.

'Around two hundred men, they entered at the east end of the village,' Redfern informed him, not wasting any time with unnecessary words. They had served together for years now and Redfern was the man Richard would always choose to be by his side.

As quickly as possible, Richard gathered his men and together they rode out through the village, ready to face the attackers. Not once did he hesitate, even though they were only thirty against two hundred. He had faced worse odds before, and today he was fighting for Hetty's safety as well as the people of Cidade Velha do Douro.

'To victory,' Redfern said, his expression grim.

'Victory,' Richard repeated, before he lifted his sword, slashed it down with force and then led the charge, spurring his horse forward to meet the enemy.

Chapter One

1816

'I'm sorry, miss. I can't take you any further. They'll have my job if I do.'

Hetty smiled brightly, forcing down the panic that welled inside her. 'You have been kind enough already,' she said, slipping from the seat next to the coachman before reaching up to help Noah down.

'It is only about two miles in that direction. If you follow the road you'll get there in no time.'

Taking the bag the coachman handed down, Hetty nodded, looking off to where he pointed. It might only take her half an hour to walk the two miles to Farnleigh Hall, but Noah was only two and a half. His little legs tired easily and she would not be able to carry him all the way. This was her problem, though, not the coachman's, who had already taken her further than the last of her money paid for.

'Thank you,' she said, gripping Noah's hand so he did not run out in front of the horses. 'I will not forget your kindness.'

The journey from Essex to Northumberland had been long and fraught with difficulties, not least because of the ever-dwindling funds she had in her purse. She'd had only enough money to pay for half the journey from Durham up the coast to Bamburgh, but thankfully the coachman had taken pity on the dishevelled young woman and her boisterous son and allowed them to sit up front with him for a lower fee. His kindness had almost reduced Hetty to tears and it had taken a few swigs of the bottle of cheap wine he'd offered her to settle her nerves.

Now the coach was continuing to Bamburgh itself before the last leg of its journey all the way to Edinburgh. Hetty's route took her inland, away from the beautiful coastline she had caught glimpses of whilst travelling. She could only hope that a farmer might pass with a cart and offer them a ride at least part of the way.

'What is the delay?' an imperious voice called from inside the carriage.

'No delay,' the coachman shouted, giving Hetty one last apologetic look before he spurred the horses on.

For a moment Hetty and Noah stood watching

the retreating coach. It travelled slowly, the bumpy road not allowing for speed.

'Come, my darling. We have a walk ahead of us,' Hetty said, smiling down at her son. He was the reason she kept going through every difficult situation. She wanted to give him a better life.

They had only walked a few paces when there was a rumble and then an almighty crash, followed by the sounds of horses whinnying. Hetty spun round, aghast to see the coach they had left moments before lying on its side half in a ditch, its wheels spinning.

One horse was in the ditch, the other three still tethered to the coach, straining to be let loose.

For a moment Hetty couldn't move, then an instinct that had been buried deep took over. The people inside the coach would be at the very least shaken, but there could be serious injuries, and Sam, the kind coachman who had taken pity on her, would likely have been thrown when the carriage overturned. These people needed help, and out here in the middle of nowhere there was no one else to give it to them.

'We need to run, my darling,' she said to Noah. He must have picked up on the tension in her voice for he held her hand a little tighter, but his little legs moved quickly and he trotted along beside her.

Her first duty was to her son, and she needed to

find somewhere safe to put him, where he would not be in any danger from the startled horses. One side of the road was lined with trees and Hetty found a suitable stump to sit him on, kissing him on the forehead.

'Mama needs to help the people in the carriage,' she said, looking for a flicker of understanding in his eyes. 'You will be able to see me all the time, but it is important you sit here and do not move.'

He nodded solemnly, tears welling in his eyes. Hetty took a moment to embrace him and then hurried away to the carriage, looking back every few seconds to ensure he was not following her.

There was movement as she reached the carriage, much to Hetty's relief. People stirring inside, beginning to gather themselves after the shock of the last few minutes.

Grimacing at the impractical dress she was wearing, Hetty lifted her skirts to her knees and pulled herself up so she could access the door of the carriage. There had been seven passengers alongside her and Noah, and then there was the coachman.

'Is anyone hurt in there?' Hetty asked, peering inside.

'My daughter,' a woman's panicked voice called out. 'I think it is her leg.'

There was a faint sob from a darkened corner of the carriage.

'I will help you,' Hetty said, holding the woman's eye. 'Keep your daughter still and calm for now, but I promise I will not leave you. Can anyone get out?' she asked, checking back over her shoulder again to make sure Noah was where she had left him.

There was a sudden jolt as the horses, still attached to the overturned carriage, surged forward. Hetty almost fell, gripping onto the edge of the door to steady herself.

'Yes,' a young man said, closest to her. 'I do not think I have anything more than a few bruises. Stand back and I will pull myself out.'

The man emerged from the door of the carriage looking dishevelled, his hands shaking as he dropped down to the ground.

'I'm worried about the horses,' Hetty said quietly, not wanting to panic the people within. 'If they take fright they could pull the carriage along the ditch, causing it to break up.'

'We need to set them free,' the young man agreed.

'I will do that,' Hetty volunteered, looking uneasily at the nervous beasts, their nostrils flaring and hooves stomping. She was much better with people than with animals, but this young man was broad-shouldered and his strong arms would be put to better use helping the other passengers from the carriage. 'You must help the other passengers out.'

Hetty approached the horses cautiously. The three still on the road skittered sideways as she neared and she had to slow her movements despite her heart hammering inside her chest. It took her a minute to understand how they were attached to the coach, but one by one she worked on the fastenings and released the horses. As soon as each one was free it galloped off down the road, disappearing into the distance.

The horse in the ditch was badly injured and from even a cursory glance Hetty could see it would not survive. She did not think it posed a danger to the coach or the passengers inside, but its hooves were resting close to the head of Sam, the coachman.

Cautiously, she crouched down, checking the pulse in the man's neck, a sob escaping her lips as she confirmed what she had suspected—the man was already dead. There was a deep wound on his head and his eyes were partially open, glazed over, never to see anything again.

Hetty took a moment to say a quick prayer over the dead man and then forced herself to move on. She would be of more use to the living. Soon help would arrive and hopefully someone would be able to ensure this man got a good burial, but that could not be her concern.

Straightening, she pulled herself out of the ditch, watching the young man who had lifted himself from the carriage first helping another passenger out. She gave him space to work, going over to where her son sat, watching everything with wide eyes.

She stroked his hair and pulled him into a hug. 'Not long now, my darling, you're doing ever so well. You just stay sitting there for me.'

His pudgy hands gripped her back and she was loath to break off the embrace. Only when he became distracted by the movement beyond her did she move away.

Thankfully, five of the passengers were out of the carriage now, with scrapes and bruises but largely unharmed. It was only the mother and her child who remained inside.

'I think there is a farm not far down the road, the direction we came from,' Hetty said, speaking to one of the gentlemen who had been inside the carriage. 'Perhaps you feel strong enough to go and get help?'

'Yes,' he said, grasping her arm. 'That is a good idea. The coachman...?'

Hetty shook her head, forcing back the tears that threatened to fall onto her cheeks. There would be time for crying later. Now she needed to keep control of herself and the situation.

As the carriage was almost empty Hetty pulled herself up and slipped inside. In the darkness within she saw a panicked looking woman and a child who was sobbing quietly, her face pale and drawn.

'Hello,' she said, smiling at the little girl. 'I'm Hetty. Do you think I can have a look at your leg?'

The little girl nodded, but flinched in anticipation of the pain as Hetty came closer. Broken limbs were one of the injuries Hetty was skilled at assessing from her time on the Peninsular. The injuries had often been severe and multiple, sustained from horses falling on their riders or the trampling of advancing or retreating troops. Here she could see the initial bruising starting to develop. There was a slight curve to the leg where there shouldn't be but, to Hetty's relief, the bone had not pierced the skin.

'I think it is broken,' Hetty said quietly to the girl's mother. 'But it has not come through the skin and with some good medical care it can be set and will heal.' Hetty turned to the little girl. 'What is your name?'

'Rose.'

'Do you think you can help me and your mama to get you out of here?'

She nodded, her eyes wide.

Hetty lifted herself up, poking her head out to speak to the passengers outside, explaining what she needed from them. The two men positioned themselves to lift Rose out, one of the women went to sit with Noah and the other started scouring the area for long, straight pieces of wood.

It took five minutes to lift Rose out of the carriage, and by that time the man who had run off to fetch help had returned with a local farmer and a cart. Hetty took her time positioning Rose in the back of the cart and then building a splint to keep the young girl's leg secure for the journey into Bamburgh. Only when she was satisfied that nothing would injure the leg further did she sit down beside her, cradling Noah between her legs. Rose's mother was on the other side, holding her child's hand.

The rest of the passengers would wait for help and organise the removal of the coachman's body. The farmer assured them it was only a short journey to Bamburgh, so it would not be long before help could be summoned, even if no one came along the road before that.

Hetty let out a long breath, holding Noah close to her. Although she had used her medical skills these last few years, there had been nothing dramatic to occupy her. This disaster had taken her back to the time she had spent in the field hospitals at the edges of the battlefields, the constant threat of violence so close, making everything seem even more pressing. It took a while for her heartbeat to slow and the feeling of being on edge to subside.

There were a hundred issues that needed his attention back at Farnleigh Hall, but this morning Richard had not been able to focus. The life he'd led these past eighteen months as a landowning earl was very different to his years in the army. It had been hard to adjust to a life lived in one place rather than constantly on the move, and sometimes he felt claustrophobic even though Farnleigh Hall was vast in size with spacious rooms, far more so than the tiny tents he had lived in for months on end whilst his regiment was progressing across Europe.

As always, a ride across the fields had cleared his head and he had pushed his horse until they had reached the cliffs overlooking the crashing waves of the North Sea. There they had rested a while before turning back and making their way to the road at a more sedate pace. He likely would not be back at Farnleigh Hall before lunch, but his time was his own even if there were many demands for his attention. That at least was something he did not miss from the army—even as an officer he had often been at the whims of higher command, awaiting their orders before he could pass them on to his men.

As he reached the road he heard the thunder of hooves coming towards him and he moved to the side, expecting a messenger to fly past on the back of a horse. Instead, three horses whipped past, nostrils flaring and manes flying out behind them in the wind. There was no rider in sight and for a moment he contemplated what was best to do. Making quick decisions was another skill honed on the battlefields and before the horses had rounded the bend he spurred his own horse after them. He rode at a distance for a while, assuming that unless they took fright the runaway animals would eventually calm down and slow, and after a couple of minutes he was rewarded. One by one the horses slowed to a trot and then came to a stop, breathing heavily after their dash along the country lane.

Richard dismounted, securing his own horse before approaching the others. He was good with animals, with horses in particular. On the battlefield having an affinity with your horse could mean the difference between life and death.

Once he had all three rogue animals under control he tied them to nearby trees, ensuring they could not cause havoc whilst he was gone. He remounted and rode back in the direction he had come, to investigate where the three runaway horses had come from and why they were so panicked.

After ten minutes he rounded a bend in the road and saw an awful sight. A carriage had overturned and lay damaged in the ditch. One horse was still attached, the leather of the bridle pulled taut as it had struggled. There was also the lifeless form of a man in the ditch, wearing the uniform of a coachman. A group of people stood close by, looking stunned, and as he approached they turned to him with desperation in their eyes.

For a moment he felt a wave of panic threaten to overwhelm him. In his mind, pictures of the dead scattered across the battlefield at Waterloo played over, but thankfully this time he was able to get control of himself before they made him lose all reason.

'Is anyone else hurt?' he asked as he slowed his horse and then dismounted.

One of the men motioned to where a farmer's cart was just about to disappear around a bend in the road. There were a few people sitting upon it and his gaze went first to a little girl who looked as though she had been crying.

As his eyes landed on the other occupants of the cart his breath caught in his throat. There was a woman sitting to one side of the girl, with a small child cradled between her legs. He only saw her for an instant, but for that instant he thought it was *her*. His Hetty. The woman he had once loved more than life itself, and then lost so soon after he had found her.

Then the cart was gone, disappearing around the corner. Richard shook himself. It wasn't the first time he'd thought he had seen her. A face in the crowd or a flash of recognition when he rode past someone. It had been a frequent occurrence in those first few painful weeks and months, but time did heal all wounds, even the emotional ones, and in the last year it had only happened a handful of times. Yet when it did it brought back every single moment of the heartbreak he had felt.

'She's dead,' he murmured to himself. Later he could wallow in his grief some more, but right now these people needed his help.

With one last look at the road where the cart had disappeared, he turned back to the passengers of the overturned coach, his mind already focused on making a plan to get them to safety and ensure the body of the coachman was recovered and the fatally injured horse dealt with.

Chapter Two

The sun broke through the clouds as they rounded the curve in the drive and set eyes upon Farnleigh Hall. It was a grand house, built of red brick with white stone around the windows and doors. Set in acres of beautiful gardens, it was a long walk from the road to the house.

Hetty wanted to turn around and flee. Only the heavy, tired footsteps of her son beside her made her press on. He deserved more than this, more than she could give him. They were alone in the world now, and it was not an easy place to be as a woman with a child.

The estate was in a beautiful part of the country and as they walked she remembered Richard lying on the narrow cot in the field hospital, telling her about his home as she'd bandaged his leg in the middle of the night. His language had always been poetic, the result of a good education and a sharp intelligence that did not have any other outlet at the periphery of the muddy battlefield. Many times, he had spoken about the hills rolling away to the sea in the distance, the sense of vastness in the landscape, the colours of the meadows and the woodland that were different to anywhere else in the world.

Tears filled her eyes at the memory and for a panicked moment she wondered if Richard would be home here at Farnleigh Hall, but dismissed the idea. It was not his home any longer. The youngest of four brothers, he had never been under the illusion that there would be any of the family property or fortune coming his way. He had set out to make his own way in the world and had succeeded—a decorated officer in the army, he had been instrumental to the victories won on the Continent. She suspected he was still in the army, still travelling abroad somewhere. It would be highly unlikely that he was visiting Farnleigh Hall at the same time she had come to Northumberland.

Hetty paused before she approached the front door, leaning down to straighten Noah's shirt and wipe a smudge of dirt from his face. He looked up at her with adoring eyes. It broke her heart to think how much trust he had in her, how he was content in the knowledge that she would always keep him safe. At two and a half he did not know they were destitute. All he needed in life right now were her arms and a regular supply of food.

With a shaking hand she knocked and took a step back. The door opened almost immediately and she was greeted by a smiling footman who took in her dishevelled appearance and the young boy at her side but did not immediately dismiss her.

'I have come to see the Earl of Farnleigh.'

'Is he expecting you?' The footman spoke with a broad Northumberland accent as he looked quizzically between her and Noah.

'No. I am hoping he will give me a few minutes of his time. I used to know his brother.'

The footman glanced back over his shoulder, looking undecided. Clearly, in a house such as this someone who looked as poor as Hetty was expected to approach through the servants' quarters, but if she entered that way she doubted she would ever actually get to see the Earl.

'Please,' she said, feeling tears welling in her eyes. The journey had been long and arduous and if the Earl refused to see her she would be stranded in a part of the country she did not know with no money and no way to support herself or Noah.

The footman's expression softened and he looked over his shoulder. 'I can ask if he'll see you, miss. What name shall I give?' He stepped back and looked down at Noah. 'I expect you're hungry. Why don't I take you both down to the kitchen to wait? I'm sure there will be a nice slice of cake or a biscuit for you.'

He led the way to the back of the house and down a set of stairs to the passages that ran under the house. There were signs of activity, but no one was rushing about as Hetty had always imagined to be the case in the underbelly of the great houses.

'You sit here and I will go and see if the Earl can see you.'

'Thank you,' Hetty said, feeling her body sag in relief as an older woman bustled over with a plate of biscuits fresh from the oven, proffering one to Noah.

'The master loves a biscuit with his tea in the afternoon, but he won't be able to manage all of these. You'd better help him out,' she said, beaming at Noah and offering the plate to Hetty.

Hetty hadn't eaten for the last twelve hours and she felt her tummy rumble at the prospect of food, but her apprehension about the upcoming meeting stopped her from taking one. The last thing she wanted was to vomit on the boots of the Earl as she asked him for charity.

'I forgot to take your name, miss,' the footman said, returning with a sheepish grin.

'It's Mrs Fairweather,' Hetty said, swallowing hard as the footman motioned for her to follow him.

'The Earl said he would see you anyway. He's in a good mood today.'

That bode well for her request for aid. She had only known Richard for a short time, an intense few weeks that, despite their brevity, had been the most memorable of her whole life. He had often spoken of his family, told her of the happy childhood he had spent in Northumberland with his three older brothers, romping through the countryside, him always running to keep up with them. The eldest, the man she was going to meet in a few minutes, was George. Richard had described him as kind and fair and level-headed. She hoped this was true—that he would listen to her story and consider her request instead of throwing her out onto the street.

Hetty felt her hands begin to shake as they approached the door leading to the Earl's study. Their whole future hung in the balance; their very existence depended on the next few minutes.

The footman opened the door and then stood to one side, announcing, 'Mrs Fairweather to see you, my lord.'

Richard spun as Whitely, the young footman he was training up, opened the door and announced the mysterious visitor.

His eyes went first to the small boy with dark hair

and bright blue eyes who stepped into the room, holding a biscuit in one hand, crumbs tumbling from his lips. There was something familiar about the boy but he could not quite place him. Then his heart crashed in his chest and his legs threatened to buckle underneath him as he saw the woman standing beside him.

Richard grabbed hold of one of the shelves on a nearby bookcase to steady himself. He was not a superstitious man, he hardly believed in the heaven and hell the local vicar spoke of during the Sunday sermon, and he certainly did not believe in ghosts. Yet standing here before him was a dead woman.

'Richard...' Hetty said, looking almost as shocked as he felt. 'It can't be.'

'You're dead.' She clearly was not dead, but he could not understand how the woman he had loved so intensely for those few weeks in Portugal could be standing here before him. 'I saw your body.'

With wide eyes Hetty shook her head. 'You thought I was dead?' Her body seemed to sag before him and he saw the colour drain from her face.

Richard crossed the room in quick strides, arriving at Hetty's side and instantly guiding her to one of the chairs that was placed on the other side of his huge desk. As his hand brushed against her lower back he felt a spark pass through him. She certainly was flesh and bone beneath the layers of clothes.

'I saw your body after the skirmish. You were dead, Hetty.'

She shook her head, at a loss as to what to tell him.

There had been a surprise attack a few days before the gathered British, Portuguese and Spanish troops were due to march inland, following the path of the Douro River to meet the bulk of Napoleon's force in Spain. It had only been a small force that had attacked Cidade Velha do Douro, but they were unprepared and the troops had to scramble to respond. After an hour of fighting they drove Napoleon's men back, but there had been much damage done to the village. The church where Richard had spent weeks recuperating had been set alight and the patients inside massacred.

'You were lying in a bloody pile next to Mr Mortimer the surgeon and some of the patients you cared for.'

'I don't remember,' Hetty said, clutching the small boy to her. He wriggled and climbed onto her lap, clearly sensing his mother's distress. 'When I regained consciousness I was surrounded by the dead and the village was deserted.'

Richard sucked in a deep breath, realising he had abandoned her, left her in a truly vulnerable state.

But he had been convinced she was dead and, heartbroken, he had thrown himself into pursuing the men responsible and leading his cavalry regiment to meet Napoleon's troops inland.

'Hetty, I'm sorry,' he said, reaching out to touch her. His fingers barely grazed her skin before she flinched at the contact and he quickly moved away, turning to hide how much her reaction hurt. Their affair had only lasted a few brief weeks but it had been intense and all-consuming, yet she was acting as if they were complete strangers.

'The footman said you were the Earl.' Hetty spoke quietly, and as Richard turned back he realised that she had expected to see George sitting behind the big desk, not him.

'My brothers died. All of them.' He gave a mirthless laugh. 'I returned home from the war to find all three of my older brothers were dead within a couple of years of each other.' It had been devastating news. Richard had been used to being part of a large, loving family and no amount of wealth or the vast estates he had inherited could make up for the loss of his brothers.

'You're the Earl?'

He nodded, realising with a rush of disappointment that it wasn't him Hetty had come to see.

'You wished for an audience with my brother?'

'I thought you would still be in the army. I had no way of contacting you.'

Richard felt his head spin. He couldn't get his thoughts straight. One part of him wanted to gather Hetty in his arms and forget about everything that had happened in the last couple of years. Surely nothing mattered but the fact that she was well and they were reunited. The other part of him, the more sensible part, urged caution. Hetty had not come to Northumberland seeking a reunion. She had not sought him out in the years between the attack on the Portuguese village and now. Her aim today had been to come and see his brother, not him. He needed to be cautious, even when his heart wanted nothing more than to embrace the woman in front of him.

Slowly his attention turned to the boy who had climbed into his mother's lap. Richard inhaled sharply as he realised why he looked so familiar.

'Who is this, Hetty?' he asked, trying to keep his voice as calm and welcoming as possible. The boy was young and no doubt the journey here had been tiring and he looked up at Richard warily.

He didn't need her to answer. The child was an exact replica of his brother James. There was a certain shape to the lips, the curve of the cheeks and above all else the startlingly blue eyes every male in the Westbridge family had possessed for the last fifty years.

'This is Noah,' Hetty said, her voice cracking as she spoke. 'My son.'

Her eyes came up and met his and Richard gave a short, sharp nod. The boy did not know of Richard or the story of his origin and right now Hetty did not wish for him to be enlightened. Richard was not a cruel man. He would not want to say anything to upset the child, even if it meant delaying hearing the truth.

Richard took a couple of steps back and leaned against the edge of his desk. It was filled with papers, but suddenly what had been important this morning paled into insignificance. Hetty was alive. These last few years he had mourned her quietly. There had been no one to share his grief with, no one in his current life who had known her. The world had kept moving forward, but he had felt as if a part of him was forever stuck in Portugal, desperate to hold the woman he loved one last time.

Rousing himself, he stood and walked closer to Hetty and Noah and then crouched down so he was at eye level with the boy.

'Hello, Noah,' he said, smiling. Noah regarded him with a serious expression before snuggling back into his mother a little further. 'My name is Richard.

Did I see you had one of my cook's famous biscuits? They're delicious, aren't they?'

Noah looked down at his hands, where there were only a few crumbs left, sticking to pudgy fingers, and then nodded.

'Shall we see if there are any more left? Then perhaps you might like to have a play on the lawn whilst I talk to your mother.'

Richard held out a hand, feeling a rush of affection as Noah reached out and took it, before jumping down from his mother's lap and allowing Richard to lead him away.

'Mama come too,' he said, looking back over his shoulder.

'Yes, I'm coming too,' Hetty said. Richard heard the catch in her voice, the emotion she was desperately trying to hide from her son.

Chapter Three

Hetty sipped at the cup of tea, glad of the generous spoonful of sugar the maid had added when serving. She needed something to settle her nerves, although she did not think even hard liquor would help her recover from the shock of today.

Noah was playing happily on the perfectly manicured lawn at the back of the house. The footman who had admitted them earlier had been pressed into service and was now running around with the little boy, chasing him and making him squeal in delight. It was a relief to see him so happy, so entertained. These last few weeks it had been just her and Noah and although she had tried her hardest to keep him occupied, there were only so many games she could play with no resources whilst constantly on the move.

Cautiously, Hetty turned her eyes to Richard and felt her heart lurch inside her chest. She had not thought to find him here at Farnleigh Hall. He had made it clear that although his brother loved and supported him, the house where he'd grown up was no longer his home. Yet she had arrived to be introduced to the Earl and it was Richard sitting in the throne-like seat behind the imposing desk.

She felt a swell of guilt. For two and a half years Noah had been on this earth and never once had she tried to contact Richard to tell him of his son. Of course there were mitigating factors—she had thought Richard had abandoned her, gone about his duty in the army and put all thoughts of her from his mind. Added to that was the reappearance of her husband. Despite Noah being conceived during her affair with Richard, because he was born whilst she was married to her husband he was considered her husband's child in the eyes of the law. Phillip Fairweather was not a forgiving man. He had made her suffer for her unwitting infidelity and Hetty had spent two years fearing for the safety of both herself and Noah. It would have been foolish to endanger them more by trying to contact Richard.

'Noah is my son,' Richard said, looking at her with the same piercing blue eyes she saw on Noah every day.

'Noah is your son,' she confirmed quietly. They were sitting on the terrace just behind the house and as long as they spoke quietly there was no risk of Noah hearing.

'He does not know?' For a man who had just found out he was a father, Richard was surprisingly calm, yet Hetty could see the subtle signs of tension. The occasional clench of his jaw, the flex of his fingers on his lap. He had always been a man who was in control, no matter the situation, and she could see that had not changed.

'No.'

He drummed his fingers on the arm of his chair. Hetty felt herself shift uncomfortably. They had so much to say to one another, but it was impossible to know where to start.

'You did not come to see me today; you thought you would find my brother. What was it you came to ask him?'

Exhaling slowly, Hetty looked up and met Richard's gaze. He was a direct man. She wondered if it came from his years in the army, where precision and clarity were so important, or if it had always been in his nature to be that way. Their affair had been intense but short-lived and afterwards she had realised that she knew little about him.

'Perhaps I can tell you what happened after the attack on Cidade Velha do Douro?'

'I think that would be a very good idea.'

Hetty felt a cold sweat start on her brow and travel through her body as she forced herself back to the little village in Portugal.

'When the French forces attacked I was helping Mr Mortimer with an amputation. At first, we were so engrossed in the work we did not notice the sounds of the skirmish outside. Only when they burst into the church did we realise what was happening. Mr Mortimer did not wish to abandon his patient, but we could hear the screams of the men being massacred as they lay helpless on their hospital cots. As the troops got closer, Mr Mortimer told me to run.'

Hetty closed her eyes at the memory of the pure fear she had felt in that moment. In the course of the war, the months she had spent traipsing after the army as her husband had insisted, she had seen many horrors, but mostly she had been a witness only after the violence. This time she'd been caught in the middle of it—and she had been acutely aware of what the French troops did to any women they captured.

She did not have to explain that fear to Richard, she could see he understood. The horrors of war had been part of his life for much longer.

'I tried to escape out of the side entrance into the courtyard but I tripped and fell down the stairs. I think I must have hit my head.' She gave a mirthless laugh. 'It was a blessing really. Whilst I lay unconscious, the French massacred everyone in the church. They must have thought I was dead for they left me where I had fallen.'

'And that was where I saw you, lying in the courtyard of the church,' Richard said, and she could hear the anguish in his voice.

'Yes, I suppose it was.' She pushed away thoughts of what could have been if Richard had just taken a few steps closer, checked she was actually dead. She would not blame him for that.

'When I woke, the village was deserted, only the dead remained. The locals had been killed or fled into the hills. There was no one there.'

This was the moment that plagued her nightmares. The memory of waking up to find piles of the dead, completely alone in the village, wandering and not knowing what to do next.

'In the end I left Cidade Velha do Douro and walked upriver. I knew there was another village a few miles away and thankfully they had been spared the massacre. Whilst trying to arrange a passage home, I discovered my husband was not dead after all. From his drunken ramblings over the years, I gather he had deserted his regiment in the confusion of battle, but life outside the army was not easy, not in a foreign country, and so eventually he handed himself in and made up a story about being injured and left behind.'

'You were reunited,' Richard said.

They hadn't spoken much about her husband. Hetty had thought him dead six months by the time she had met Richard, but she had hinted at what sort of man he was.

'We were. Then I found out I was pregnant. Phillip was horribly angry, and when he was discharged from the army and we returned to England he threatened to put me out onto the street, but I think he liked having power over me.'

'Noah thinks Mr Fairweather is his father?'

Hetty nodded. 'He did. Phillip died a few months ago. He left nothing but debts and his family refused to support me and Noah.' She shrugged. 'We are, quite literally, penniless. I used the last of the little money I had on the coach fare here and for much of our journey we had to rely on the kindness of strangers to share their food.'

She took a deep breath and then looked Richard in the eye. 'I came to ask your brother for help. I hoped you might have spoken of me to him and he might take pity. You always said he was kind and fair.'

For a long moment Richard was silent, mulling over her words in his mind. She used to love that about him, how he would look at a problem from all angles before coming to a decision on how best to deal with it.

'I thought you were dead,' he said slowly, holding up his hands as if in an act of confession. 'Granted I should have been more careful in ascertaining that you were actually dead, but I truly believed it. You knew I was alive. I can understand why you could not contact me whilst your husband was alive, but you did not come to Northumberland to seek me out…'

'I thought you had left me,' Hetty said quietly. 'Our time together in Portugal was short and I didn't know you, not really. I thought you had decided it was time to move on. You would not be the first officer to leave a woman behind once he'd got his orders.'

Richard pressed his lips together and Hetty could tell he was trying hard not to say something he might regret. Although it was heartening to know he had not willingly left her, it did not matter now. Too much had happened in the intervening years. They could not just pick up where they had left off. She knew in her heart that Richard was a good man, she just had to hope he would agree to support Noah in some way.

Richard was trying his hardest not to show his anger. He prided himself of always being in control of his emotions and today, despite its myriad challenges, would be no different.

Hetty's cool, detached manner hurt, he could not deny it. She had not come seeking him out and she did not seem particularly pleased to see him. Whatever had burned so intensely between them three years earlier, that was not the reason she was here. He needed to push aside thoughts of a loving reunion and focus on what was really important: their son.

'What support were you hoping for from my brother?'

Hetty's composure wavered for a second and he thought he caught a glimpse of the fear and desperation beneath. He softened slightly, telling himself that she had not had an easy couple of years. It was perhaps not unexpected that she kept herself so distant.

She gave a little mirthless laugh. 'Anything.' Leaning forward in her chair, she dropped her voice, as if even admitting what she said next was dangerous. 'We have nothing, apart from the clothes we wear. Our only alternative is begging on the streets or going to the workhouse.'

Richard inhaled sharply at the thought. He could see tears glistening in Hetty's eyes and realised she was not exaggerating. These last few months she had feared for the life and the future of her beloved son, and that fear weighed heavily upon her.

Leaning forward, he reached out a hand and placed it on hers, withdrawing it quickly when she flinched at the contact. Trying to ignore how much the rejection even of this simple sign of affection hurt, he forced himself to temper the gruffness of his voice.

'You will stay here as my guests, for now. Over the coming weeks we can work out the details. I would like to spend some time with my son, to get to know him.'

'We do not need to impose on your hospitality,' Hetty said quickly. 'We are quite used to humble lodgings, if you could just give us enough to fund them for a month or two.'

Richard shook his head. On this he would not be moved. 'No. You will stay here.' He stood, his head finally clearing. 'I will let it be known that you are a distant relative, fallen on hard times. That should satisfy the local gossips. Then it will not be viewed as strange for me to spend time with Noah.'

'You wish to get to know him?'

'He is my son, Hetty. Whatever has passed between us, whatever cannot be undone, I will not let him suffer another moment of hardship.'

He saw the tears fall onto her cheeks and stopped his pacing, kneeling down beside her.

'You have done your best in difficult circumstances, but things need not be difficult any longer. I know I cannot claim him as mine, but I will provide for him whatever he needs.'

'You won't take him away from me?' Hetty said, her voice so quiet he barely heard the words.

'No. Never. A child needs their mother. How could you ask such a thing?'

Hetty shrugged. 'It was always Phillip's threat. That he would turn me out but keep Noah…and without me to protect him…'

'I am not your late husband, and I am not a cruel man. You will stay with Noah.' He pushed away the pain he felt from hearing her words. He had thought she knew him better than that, but perhaps the price of the hardship of the intervening years had been her faith in humanity.

'Thank you,' she said, giving her first proper smile since she had arrived in his study an hour earlier.

Chapter Four

Hetty sank under the surface of the water, fully submerging herself as she let the bubbles escape from her mouth, and wondered if she was dreaming. Baths were a luxury she had not experienced in a long time. At least not a bath such as this. A huge steaming tub of water had been placed in front of the fireplace, although today the warm temperature outside meant there was no need for a fire burning in the grate. It was quite a contrast with the shallow few inches of water she had been allowed in the cold metal tub, barely having time to get herself clean before she was ordered out by Phillip.

Three maids had brought the water in buckets up the stairs and poured it into the tub whilst chattering away cheerfully. A fourth maid had sprinkled in something that smelled of lavender and then returned with an armful of clothes.

'Lord Westbridge apologises for the age and style

of the dresses, but there has been no lady in residence since his mother passed away.'

'These are for me?' Hetty had asked as the maid laid out four dresses that would have been at the height of fashion twenty years earlier. 'I don't want to impose. I can just wear this.'

The maid had crinkled her nose a little and assured Hetty that her own dress would be cleaned and dry as soon as possible.

That had been half an hour earlier, just before she had stepped into the bath. At first, she'd had the urge to scrub herself quickly and then get out. It felt odd to actually just sit and do nothing, but as her body began to relax she realised quite how exhausted the last few weeks had left her. There was the physical tiredness, of course, born from the miles she had walked, often carrying Noah when his legs had grown too weary, but there was also an emotional fatigue. Months of worrying where their next meal would come from and whether the trip to Northumberland would be successful, the threat of complete destitution never far from her mind.

It would take more than one bath to cure all that, but as Hetty allowed the warmth to suffuse her body she felt a weight lift from her.

Richard was a good man. Even though she had not known him long, she could be certain of that.

He had been beloved by the men who'd followed him loyally and spoke of a close relationship with his family. She could see he was earnest in his desire to get to know Noah, to be part of his son's life even if he could not claim him as his legitimate heir. She thought too that he was truthful when he promised not to send her away.

It was not the solution she had come looking for, but perhaps, for Noah at least, it was even better.

A little voice deep inside piped up, asking, *And what about you?*

Hetty closed her eyes. How easy it would be if she could fall for Richard once again, and he for her. He had loved her once, she was certain of that, and she had loved him, but there was now a gulf between them that she did not think even his kindness could bridge.

These last few years she had been badly treated, not only by Phillip but also by his family. They had all known of her infidelity and chosen to believe Phillip's account that painted her as an unfaithful wife who had the audacity to fall pregnant by her lover whilst Phillip was wounded in battle. She'd had no way out, no family she could flee to, no money of her own. Phillip and his mother had controlled every aspect of her life.

Richard was right when he said he was not like

her late husband, but that did not matter any more. Hetty could not believe that she would be able to trust anyone ever again.

Finally, she rose from the bath, stepping out and drying herself before inspecting the dresses the maid had left out for her. She had been given instructions to ring when she needed help dressing, but the very idea was foreign to Hetty. She had grown up in a respectable household where they had employed a maid who had helped with everything from preparing food to tending the chickens, but in the last few years she had done everything herself.

It was only when she tried to begin fastening the first of the dresses that she realised these garments were so much more complicated and intricate than anything she had ever worn before. With a groan she gave up and rang the bell.

'You're out of the bath, miss,' the maid said when she bustled in. 'Oh, that is a lovely gown to be sure. Shall I help you with the fastenings at the back?'

'Yes, please, Sarah,' Hetty said, smiling at the friendly maid.

'We'll have you done up in no time at all. I expect you want to see what that lovely boy of yours is up to. He has the most adorable laugh.'

'He is playing in the nursery?'

'Yes. He's quite happy if you want to rest for a while, or I can organise some tea.'

'That is very kind, but I think I will go and check on Noah.'

'Very good, miss. Just ring if you need anything. Lord Westbridge asked me to act as your lady's maid until something more permanent can be arranged.'

Hetty took a moment to assess herself in the mirror that hung on the wall. She had brushed out her hair and currently it hung damp to well past her shoulders. Her face was thin, more angular than it used to be, but that came from months of poor sustenance. Quickly she looked away. It did not matter what she looked like. She was not trying to impress anyone.

After much debate, she and Richard had agreed that Noah would have one of the bedrooms in the nursery on the third floor of Farnleigh Hall and that she would take one of the modest rooms alongside. He had offered her a choice of bedrooms, even showing her some grand rooms on the first floor, but she felt more comfortable here. It also meant if Noah woke scared in the night it would not be far for him to travel to find her bed to clamber into.

Making her way along the short corridor, she heard laughter, her son's happy giggle that she realised she had not heard for weeks. He had been quiet whilst they were travelling, stoical as much as a small child could be. He'd withdrawn into himself, speaking less, smiling less, and it warmed Hetty's heart to hear his laughter now.

'Reporting for duty, sir.' Richard's voice rang out and as Hetty peeked round the doorframe she saw him on the floor, toy soldier in one hand and horse in the other.

'Horses can't speak,' Noah said, giggling almost uncontrollably.

'No, you've got it wrong. Humans can't speak and horses can,' Richard said, moving the horse as if it were talking.

Noah rolled back, holding his belly and laughing. Then he caught sight of Hetty by the door.

'Richard says horses can talk,' he said, giggling again. 'But that's silly.'

She hadn't expected to see Richard on the floor, playing. He was an earl, a man with myriad responsibilities. Yet here he was, making the first step in getting to know the son she had denied him the last few years.

She felt a pang of regret. The rational part of her knew she'd had no choice. When Phillip had returned from the dead, she had lost her autonomy and her ability to make any decisions about her or Noah's future. Still, she allowed herself a moment to imagine how things could have been different if Noah had been born into a household where love, not fear, abounded.

'Did you enjoy your bath?'

'I did, thank you. I had not realised how much grime I had accumulated these last few weeks. It feels good to wash that all away.' Her fingers grazed against the material of the borrowed dress. 'Thank you for the loan of the dress.'

'I am just sorry there is not something that is a better fit. I can ask the modiste from Bamburgh to visit in the coming days.'

'There really is no need. Sarah has taken my dress...'

'I told her to burn it.'

'Burn it?' She felt a flicker of disbelief flare inside her.

'Yes. You had been travelling in it for weeks. It could not be saved.'

'Of course it could. A good scrub and it would have been fine.'

He looked at her with a quizzical expression. 'I did not think the disposal of a ragged old dress would cause so much consternation.'

'It was *my* dress,' she said through gritted teeth.

'I will buy you a new one.'

'That is not the point.' She felt anger swell and

flare. For so long she had been helpless and voiceless. Trapped in her own home by a husband who despised her and threatened her with the streets and separating her from her son. These last few months had been difficult, but she had finally felt free. It had been similar to how she had felt when she'd thought Phillip dead and she'd worked as a nurse in Portugal. Every decision made was her own.

'You cannot just dictate everything. It was my dress. My decision as to whether it gets burnt or washed.'

Richard eyed her for a minute before standing up. 'I will be back, Noah. Set up the troops and choose a leader who is not a talking horse.'

Noah got to work, oblivious of the tension rippling between his parents.

'May I have a word in private?' Richard said, his voice clipped but polite.

He led her out of the nursery to an alcove with a window seat that looked out over the gardens below.

'There is clearly something here I do not understand,' Richard said.

'You ordered my dress to be burned. What is there not to understand? It was unreasonable.'

He shrugged. 'I did not want fleas in my house.'

'I do not have fleas.'

'You've been travelling for weeks, staying no

doubt in less than salubrious accommodation. There is a fair chance there were fleas in your clothing.'

'It was all I had.'

'In a few days you will have a whole wardrobe of dresses, and until then you can borrow what you need.'

He made it all sound so reasonable. Hetty was sure she had not been carrying fleas in her dress, but she could not deny it had been in need of a good wash. After travelling for weeks, the hem was filthy and the colour much duller than it had once been. Yet it should have been her decision to get rid of it, not his.

'I will not have another man tell me what I may keep and what must be destroyed, what I can do and what is forbidden,' she said, her voice low but dangerous. Never again would she allow a man to have that power over her.

Richard looked as though he was going to argue and then something softened in his eyes. He reached out to take her hand and for a moment it was as if the last three years had disappeared. Hetty could almost feel the warmth of the sun on her face as they strolled by the edge of the Douro, dreaming of a better future.

Then Richard's fingers met hers and the contact made her crash back to the present. Her muscles tensed and her whole body seized up, ready to run or fight. His touch was momentary, fleeting, but Hetty felt as if her heart might explode out of her chest it was pounding so hard.

She saw the pain in his eyes as he quickly pulled away. Whatever had happened these last few years, it was clear he still held some affection for her and she had just acted as if his touch was repugnant. She wanted to explain, to tell him how much her heart and mind had been tortured since he had seen her last, but the words would not come.

Chapter Five

Richard wiped his brow before parrying and going in for the next attack.

Wooden sword clashed upon wooden sword and Noah squealed in delight. After a few moments of tapping their swords together, Richard allowed Noah to land a blow on his torso and groaned theatrically.

'You have me, Sir Noah. You have bested me in combat.'

'Sir Noah wins!' Noah shouted in delight. 'Fight again!'

Richard guided the boy to a bench and they sat, both panting from the exertion.

'Alas, I have work to do, but we shall fight again tomorrow, and I will not be so easily bested then,' Richard said. It was only mid-morning but he had stripped down to his shirtsleeves as he'd played with his son. The weather was warm even for July and the sun was relentlessly beating down.

'You're very good with him,' Hetty said as she appeared from one of the paths that led into the formal gardens. They had not spoken since the day before, when they'd argued about the fate of her dress. Richard had spent the evening distracted from his work, trying to make sense of her reaction to him when he'd reached out to touch her. It had been an innocent gesture, one that he had hoped would convey that he understood the situation was difficult for her. Despite this, Hetty had reacted as if his touch had burned her.

'My brothers always played with me. I have their example to guide me. I was never bored as a child, never left alone for long. At least not until the second youngest went away to school. Then the house seemed horribly quiet.'

Hetty came and sat beside them on the bench and Richard smiled when Noah climbed up into her lap. He wondered if he would ever be able to comfort his son as Hetty did, knowing it was far too early to answer that question. There were many things to be resolved first, not least their living arrangements. For a few weeks, or a month, they could stay as his guests and no one would think much of the widow and her son who had sought refuge at Farnleigh Hall, but he was unmarried and if the arrangement went on too long there would be gossip and rumours he did not want to subject either Hetty or Noah to.

There were a few possible solutions, but it was too early to broach them as yet. He had to tell himself not to rush things. The orderly part of him wanted to get everything sorted this very instant, to have the future settled, but he knew where other people's lives were involved, he had to take things more slowly.

'I wonder if we might talk,' Hetty said, looking up at him from under her dark eyelashes. She looked radiant this morning, her cheeks rosy and her hair pinned into a loose bun that sat low at her neck.

'I have a few minutes, but then I must ride out to meet my land steward. There was some storm damage to one of the properties at the edge of the estate, and I also need to survey the perimeter wall at the north edge of Farnleigh.'

'Perhaps I could ride out with you. If you can spare someone to watch Noah.'

'I want to ride,' Noah said, his eyes shining at the prospect of seeing a horse.

'You are far too young,' Hetty said with an indulgent smile.

'My father put me on the back of my first pony at the age of three,' Richard said.

'I'm nearly three,' Noah said, holding up three pudgy fingers to drive the point home.

'But you're not three yet,' Hetty said softly. 'Perhaps Lord Westbridge will show you his horses one day.'

'Who is Lord Westbridge?' He stumbled a little over the name, making Richard smile.

'I am.' Richard ruffled Noah's hair, 'But you call me Richard.' He turned back to Hetty. 'I am sure there will be plenty of volunteers to watch Noah. This afternoon I will send out word that we are looking for a nursemaid and a tutor for him.'

'He doesn't need all that.'

Richard shrugged. He didn't want to get into an argument about it in front of the boy, and he realised that although it was a big adjustment for him, learning he had a son, this sudden change in circumstance would be difficult for Hetty too. He could rein himself in and tread cautiously, but he would not compromise on the end result. Noah would want for nothing.

'Shall we meet at the stables in half an hour?' Richard suggested.

'Yes. I will see if there is something I can change into.'

Half an hour later Richard stood with his horse's reins in one hand, waiting for Hetty. She had changed into an ancient riding habit that made her look like a lady from the last century, but she carried it off well.

'This is Cleopatra,' he said as he introduced her to the beautiful black mare. 'I was not sure how much riding you have done in the last few years. Cleopatra is a good-natured horse and will serve you well whatever the terrain.'

'You have a full stable, I see,' Hetty said, motioning to the rows of stalls full of horses.

'It is one of my weaknesses. I am but one man, yet I cannot seem to stop buying horses. It takes a veritable army of grooms to ensure they are well exercised each day.'

'Is this your favourite?' She motioned to the horse standing at his right shoulder.

'Yes, but don't tell the others. They might get jealous. This is Caesar.'

Hetty took a moment to stroke both the horses, admiring their glossy coats and strong physiques. He liked that about her, her assessing eye. It was one of the things that had made her invaluable as a nurse. Whatever the circumstance, she would take a moment to check everything over. She could hurry when the situation demanded it, but she would not be rushed.

He stepped behind her, catching a hint of lavender as he helped her into the saddle. Three years earlier, he had known every inch of her body. They'd had to snatch moments of privacy where they could, but their affair had been intense and intimate. He had dreamed of being able to spend one more day with her, but now she was actually here it was as if they were strangers.

Once she was seated, he stepped away and mounted Caesar, glad of the enforced distance between them.

The morning was glorious, hot and sunny without a single cloud in the sky. On horseback there was a slight breeze, but soon Richard had once more shed his jacket and rolled his sleeves up to his elbows.

They rode in silence for a few minutes, Richard allowing Hetty to get used to Cleopatra. Those first few minutes were crucial in finding the rhythm of the horse and ensuring a more comfortable ride later on.

'There are good views of the village from up here, and on a clear day you can see all the way to the coast,' Richard said as they ascended one of the many hills that made up his land.

'I caught a few glimpses of the sea on the journey up here. It looked glorious.'

'It is, at least on a day like today. It can look rather dark and unforgiving in the winter.'

They fell silent, Richard acutely aware that Hetty had asked to ride with him for a particular reason.

'I wanted to apologise for my behaviour yesterday,' she said eventually. 'In the nursery, when we were discussing my clothes.'

'There is nothing to apologise for. We were viewing the matter from different but equally valid perspectives. I thought I was doing you a kindness by getting rid of your old clothes and arranging for new ones. You saw it as an attack on your right to make your own decisions.'

'You make it all sound so reasonable,' Hetty murmured.

'I am sorry I ordered your dress to be burned without consulting you.'

'Thank you. And I am sorry I did not see it as an act that was born of kindness.' She took a deep breath. 'I am not much used to kindness.'

Richard glanced across at her. She looked so solemn, so serious, and it hurt his heart to see it.

'I am also sorry for how I reacted when you touched me,' she said, glancing over at him before looking away.

'I should not have presumed...'

'No.' She shook her head. 'I know you wished to comfort me, nothing more, but I could not help my response.'

For a moment they rode on in silence, Richard puzzling over her choice of words.

'I know you are a good man, Lord Westbridge.'

'Richard—you have always called me Richard.'

'I did back then, but everything is different now. It has to be different.'

With a clarity that pierced him like a diamond cutting through stone, he realised why Hetty had wanted to ride out with him today. She was here to ensure that he realised there would be nothing romantic between them.

'I ask nothing of you, Hetty, apart from the chance to know my son.'

'I know.' She was refusing to look at him, her eyes firmly fixed on the horizon.

He cleared his throat, trying to form a coherent thought from all those clamouring for attention in his mind.

Then she looked at him, pure anguish in her eyes. 'I did love you. In Portugal. I loved you more than I thought possible. Back then, all *this* would have been a fairytale.' She gestured to the estate around them, her arm sweep including him.

'I know,' he said softly. 'And I loved you.'

'But too much has happened. We cannot just slip back to where we were. I am a different person.'

'I have not asked that of you, Hetty,' Richard said, trying to keep his voice calm and level. She was obviously in distress, yet he could not see what had prompted this. In the twenty-four hours since she had crashed back into his life, he had not said anything to make her think he expected them to pick up where they had left off three years earlier.

'You have not,' she said, 'because you are good and noble. I do not presume to think you would still desire me in that way either—for all I know, you are planning to marry or have your heart engaged elsewhere.' Her cheeks were flushed and she was gripping the reins tightly. He could see tension pulsing through her body. 'These last few years have been torture…' She trailed off, clenching her jaw. 'I will not bore you with the details, but I find it difficult to accept kindness. And being touched makes me feel panic like I have never felt before. That is what I think you saw yesterday. I did not mean to react that way to you, but I cannot help it.'

'What did he do to you?' The question was out before he could stop it.

Hetty shook her head, tears welling in her eyes, but she quickly brushed them away. With anyone else he would have reached across, narrowed the gap between them and taken her hand in his, but he remembered her reaction from the day before and kept completely still.

She was gripping the reins hard now and Richard could see the horse was picking up on her agitation.

Cleopatra was docile and gentle, but she would get spooked if Hetty didn't relax a little soon.

'You don't have to tell me,' he said quickly, not wanting to cause her any further distress. 'And you don't need to worry. I am not expecting a romantic reunion. We had our moment three years ago. Life is different now. All I want is to get to know my son.'

She nodded but still didn't loosen her grip on the reins.

'Try to relax a little. Cleopatra is picking up on your distress,' Richard said, cursing silently as his words made Hetty tense all the more.

Before he could do anything, the normally calm horse let out a whinny and reared up. Somehow, Hetty managed to cling on, flinging herself down so she gripped around the horse's neck. Cleopatra bolted, racing off across the field. Richard spurred Caesar forward. There wasn't much he could do from a distance, but hopefully Cleopatra would calm before she flung Hetty from her back. If he could be there to take the reins it would prevent the horse from bolting again.

He leaned low, feeling the air whip past his ears, and within a minute he had drawn level with Hetty and Cleopatra.

'Come now,' he called out, speaking to the horse

rather than the woman on her back. 'That's enough—slow down now.'

It was impossible to know if it was the soothing sound of his voice that calmed the horse or if Cleopatra had just had enough of galloping, but her hooves slowed and after a few moments she came to a stop.

Richard dismounted, quickly securing Caesar to a nearby tree and then taking hold of Cleopatra's reins.

'Are you hurt?'

Hetty shook her head, her eyes wide with fright.

'Slip down. I will catch you.'

Shaking, Hetty slid from the horse into Richard's arms. This time she did not recoil at his touch. Perhaps the shock of the last few minutes had numbed her. When he tried to gently pull away, she held on to him more tightly, burying her head in his shoulder.

'You're safe now,' Richard said, tentatively raising a hand to stroke her hair. 'You're safe.'

Hetty let out a shuddering sob and he wondered if she was crying from the shock of the runaway horse or with relief at finally being somewhere safe.

As she burrowed her head deeper in his shoulder Richard had to squash down the flicker of affection he felt spark inside him. Hetty could not have made it clearer that she did not want to rekindle what they had once shared, and he did not want to push the matter. In truth, he was finding it hard, learning he had a son, someone to care for and love. Someone who could be snatched away at any moment, just like everyone else he had ever loved. It would be too much to worry about Hetty as well.

Once she had stopped shaking, she took a step back and gave him a sheepish smile. 'I'm sorry. I haven't ridden for a long time and I forgot how much a horse picks up on the temperament of its rider.'

'There is no harm done. Cleopatra is not hurt. We can lead the horses back if you would prefer.'

'What about meeting your steward?'

'He will understand.'

Hetty eyed the horses for a moment and then shook her head. 'No, if I do not get back on now, my fear will conquer me, and I refuse to be afraid any longer.'

'You wish to ride?'

'I do.'

'Then let me help you back into the saddle.'

Chapter Six

'It's the same woman—the one you were completely head over heels in love with in Portugal?' Major Redfern said as he leaned on the fence and watched the horse trot around in a circle in front of them. They had been invited to view a horse for sale on an estate a few miles south of Bamburgh and currently the grooms were trying to showcase the horse's prowess.

'The very same.'

'And she has turned up after all these years of you thinking her dead, with a boy in tow who she claims to be your son?'

'He is my son, Redfern. I knew it the moment I set eyes upon him. He looks exactly like my brother James.'

Major Alexander Redfern puffed out his cheeks and slapped Richard on the back. 'Congratulations… I suppose. When is the announcement?'

'There will be no announcement. We are not involved romantically.'

Never one for hiding his emotions, Redfern frowned. 'You were besotted and, from what I saw, she felt the same about you.'

Richard sighed. Three years ago, he would have jumped at the chance to marry Hetty. He'd been moments away from proposing when the French had attacked the village and he had led the charge against them to defend Cidade Velha do Douro, only to find his decision had cost him the woman he loved.

Redfern cleared his throat. 'Tell me to stay out of your affairs, but has this got something to do with your maudlin way of thinking that everyone good in your life is going to die?'

'No.'

'Because it's claptrap. Superstitious claptrap. Parents die, your brothers were unlucky, and this Fairweather woman wasn't actually dead after all.'

'It isn't because of that.'

'If you love her, then surely it's better to throw yourself into it. No matter what happens in five, ten or twenty years' time.'

'It isn't that.' Richard could not deny that in the last few years he had sometimes felt cursed. Everyone he had loved had died, but in his heart he knew it was nothing more than bad luck. Nevertheless, he could not deny it had affected him. Since inheriting the Earldom he had been aware of the expectation that he would marry and start producing heirs. Especially as he was the last of his line. He had put off the search for a wife, unable to bear the idea that he might open his heart to someone else, only for her to be taken away from him too. 'We are not the same people we were then.'

Redfern straightened and raised his eyebrows but didn't push any further. 'What do you think?' he said, motioning to the horse that was being paraded in front of them.

'He's strong, but he's got a slight limp. His back left hoof is paining him.'

'Yes, I thought the same. He's won three races but has tired quickly and now is out to pasture.'

'I don't think he's our stallion,' Richard said.

'No, nor do I.'

They waved at the groom, indicating their thanks for his efforts, and turned and walked away, heading back to their own horses.

'I heard something that might interest you,' Redfern said as they headed away from the stables and out to the road. 'There's a young man recently discharged from the navy just up the coast from Bamburgh. Quite badly injured. His ship caught fire and he was trapped below for some time. From what I hear, it is a miracle he survived, but the navy spat him out and his family are now desperate.'

'Where is he in his recovery?'

'I do not know. He was burned, so I am not sure.'

'I will visit,' Richard said, grimacing. Of all the injuries he had seen in ex-military men over the years, burns were by far the worst. Amputated limbs could be compensated for and a determined man could learn to function with loss of sight, but burns either killed slowly or left a man with skin so tight everything contracted and it became impossible to do even the most basic of tasks.

'Perhaps your Mrs Fairweather will be able to help him. She saved your life when you refused to have your leg cut off.'

'She did.' Richard rubbed his thigh where the wound had been. It had healed well after the infection had passed and now it only pained him if he spent a long day in the saddle. Mostly he didn't think of his injury, although sometimes he found himself walking with a slight limp. 'I do not know whether she has retained her skills. I think the last few years have not been easy for her.'

'I doubt it is something you forget. Like how to cut a man down in battle. I may not have wielded a sword for two years, but if someone launched an attack I do not think it would take long for me to remember how best to brandish a weapon.'

They came to a fork in the road and slowed their horses.

'Will you send me the address of the navy man?'

'Of course. I will also send out enquiries far and wide and let it be known we are looking for a stallion.'

'Thank you. Come for dinner next week. You can meet my son.'

Redfern raised his hat and then spurred his horse on, taking the road west whilst Richard turned north, heading home.

The ride was therapeutic. He loved his home and the rolling hills of Northumberland, but often he felt trapped by estate business. Never had he been expected to inherit, so his father had been a little lax on his education in estate matters, allowing Richard to choose subjects that interested him more. It had meant that as a boy he had spent more time reading military accounts or racing across the fields on horseback than learning how to run the estate.

That didn't mean that he neglected it now. After the initial upheaval when he had first arrived, he had worked hard to get everything in order but it had seemed hollow. Even though he had been born and raised at Farnleigh it should never have been his home as an adult and sometimes he still felt like an outsider.

Now, though, perhaps things would be different. Noah might not be his legitimate son, but he was his blood and it gave him a spark of hope for the future. He wondered if his enthusiasm for being the Earl of Farnleigh might increase, knowing Noah was there to benefit from his efforts.

Hetty stretched out on the lawn, enjoying the warmth of the sun on her face. She had spent the morning chasing Noah around the extensive gardens, playing hide and seek. After weeks spent in cramped rooms in coaching inns and the confined conditions of shared carriages, it was heavenly to have such space, for her as well as Noah.

They had been at Farnleigh Hall for three days now and it still felt like a dream. Hetty awoke each morning disorientated, still not used to the comfortable bed or the luxurious furnishings. She had eaten more in the last three days than she had in the preceding few weeks, and the food was beautifully presented and delicious.

What pleased her the most was Richard's reaction to Noah. Each day he made sure he spent some time with his son. Not too much to be overwhelming for the boy or overbearing for her, but an hour or so where he played with him or took him to explore the estate.

Yet, despite all of this, Hetty still felt an anxiety that gnawed deep inside her. Richard had promised to provide for Noah, and at present that meant they were treated as honoured guests, but she was aware the situation could not continue this way indefinitely. Richard was young but his mind would have to turn to marriage and begetting a legitimate heir one day. She doubted his wife would accept her and Noah continuing to live at Farnleigh Hall.

As always, her worries were running away from her. Right now, they were happy and safe. The future was up for negotiation. Perhaps Richard might have a small property nearby she could rent from him. Although she did not have any money at present, Hetty was not afraid of hard work. Even in the years she had been back in Essex with her husband she had not remained idle, using the skills she had picked up in the war to help the elderly or infirm. If there was no such work here she was not too proud to take in laundry or work as a maid, as long as she could ensure that Noah was cared for.

She propped herself up on one elbow and looked down at Noah's face as he napped in the shade on the blanket beside her. *He* was what was important.

As long as they were together and Noah was safe, they could survive anything.

From her spot on the blanket she saw Richard riding up the long drive towards the house. For a moment she let herself imagine what life could be like if they allowed themselves to rekindle the passion that had once flowed between them. She was not of the right social status to marry an earl, but she suspected that would not have stopped Richard if he'd felt it the right thing to do. She imagined herself as the Countess, spending her nights in Richard's bed and her days strolling the grounds with her husband, Noah playing contentedly nearby.

Then she felt a shiver travel along her spine. Part of her wanted the fantasy. A life of luxury, a more certain future for her son. Yet she knew they could not go back to the relationship they'd had before. Too much had happened and she felt like a different person now.

'Noah is resting, I see,' Richard said as he approached on his way back from the stables.

'I think the fresh air is good for him. He's been running around all morning.'

Richard smiled but there was a hint of sadness in his expression. 'I have the fondest memories of doing the same, when I was a little older, of course.'

'With your brothers?'

'Yes.'

Hetty hesitated. The question on her lips was probably too personal, yet Richard seemed to anticipate her curiosity.

'You wish to know what happened to them?'

'When we were in Portugal you were so sure you would not inherit.'

'My father always joked that our family was blessed. Many of his friends prayed for years for a single son, a single heir, and here he was with four. Certainly, his descendants should have been enough to fill all the pews in the church in a couple of generations.'

'And now there is just you.'

Richard crouched down beside Noah and stroked his hair. 'The second oldest, Henry, died first. He was always a little sickly as a child, always suffered with a bad chest. My father sent him to Europe to enjoy the warm air when he finished school, but it was there that he developed consumption. He lived a few more years but the illness claimed him when we were in Portugal.'

'I am sorry to hear it.'

'He was a clever man, always reading, always coming up with new schemes and inventions. The world is a poorer place without him.' Richard gave a tight smile that didn't reach his eyes and Hetty could see how difficult this was for him. The old Hetty would have reached out, sought to comfort him with a gentle touch, yet, despite his distress, she couldn't bring herself to do it and she hated herself a little for this lack of humanity.

'James died next. He was vibrant, full of energy and loved life. Like me, he was neither the heir nor the spare and was expected to make his own way in the world. He joined the army a year before I did and distinguished himself in battle. He was killed on the field at the Battle of Waterloo.'

'Oh, that's terrible…'

'George was the eldest, and the last to die. He was riding out to meet the woman he hoped to marry and his horse stumbled and he was thrown. He broke his neck and died instantly.'

'I am so sorry, my lord,' Hetty said, seeing Richard wince at her formality towards him. His hand rested on the blanket only a few inches away from hers, yet she still could not reach out and take it.

'The worst thing is when people congratulate me on my newfound elevation in the world. As if I should be pleased that I traded three brothers for an earldom.'

'Some people would be, I suppose.'

'Monsters.'

'After everything I saw whilst following the army,

and then helping Mr Mortimer in Portugal, I feel less trusting of people's basic humanity.'

'War turns even good men into fiends.'

'No,' Hetty said quickly. 'I do not believe that. I think the good men stay good, despite the horrific circumstances they find themselves in. Those who commit atrocities already have the seed of evil inside them.'

'This is a heavy subject for a Wednesday afternoon, Mrs Fairweather.'

Hetty swallowed hard. Despite her insistence that they observe the rules of formal society, with her eschewing his given name and using his title instead, it felt as though an arrow had just pierced her heart to hear him call her *Mrs Fairweather*. It was a reminder that for so long she had belonged to her husband, not even allowed to retain her own name alongside everything else he had taken from her.

Yet she was in no position to protest, not when she had been the one to insist they address one another so formally in the first place.

'I'm sorry. I think I grew a little maudlin as I sat here on my own. Now I have passed it on to you, which is unfair.'

'I have a proposition that might cheer you, or at least distract you.'

'I'm intrigued.'

'I have heard of a man recently discharged from the navy after a fire devastated the ship he was serving on. Apparently, he was burned quite badly. I have no doubt the navy doctors patched him up before he was discharged, but I expect the family do not have enough money to pay for a physician to visit now he is home.'

Hetty sat up a little straighter. The request was not what she had been expecting, but that did not make it unwelcome.

'I suspect you might have something to offer, even if it is just advice on caring for him, how to tend his wounds, that sort of thing.'

'What is your interest in the man?'

Richard shrugged and looked out into the distance. 'I employ a couple of ex-soldiers, men who were injured in the war and perhaps might not find employment elsewhere. I have no idea how badly this man has been injured, whether he will be looking for work one day or if he has been sent home to die, but I would like to see him.'

Hetty thought of the young footman who had first greeted them on arrival at Farnleigh Hall. When he had played with Noah whilst she and Richard talked, she had noticed a limp and she wondered if he was one of the ex-soldiers.

'I would very much like to accompany you.' Hetty

leaned over and stroked Noah's hair. 'Although I cannot leave Noah.'

'Of course. I meant to tell you I have organised for a potential nursemaid to visit later this afternoon to see if she is a good candidate for the job.'

It was difficult thinking of someone else looking after Noah and part of her wanted to rail and protest against this change, but she also knew that if she was going to one day support herself she would have to be able to leave Noah for at least part of the day with someone she trusted. Finding a nursemaid did not mean she had to relinquish the time she spent with Noah, it would just mean he was looked after even when she was occupied elsewhere.

'Thank you,' she said, trying to force a smile onto her face.

'I will inform you when she arrives. If she is suitable and can start immediately, perhaps we can plan to ride out to visit the injured man on Friday.'

'Very well.'

He smiled softly, his voice taking on a teasing note. 'Although I will not force you to ride Cleopatra all the way to Bamburgh. I am sure I can rustle up a carriage to take us there.'

Chapter Seven

Hetty stormed out of the drawing room, a bundle of dresses in her arms.

'Where is he?' she asked Whitely, the young footman who was walking through the hall, arms filled with silverware that glinted in the sunlight and smelled of silver polish.

'Lord Westbridge, miss?'

'Yes. Lord Westbridge.' She spoke through clenched teeth, reminding herself that Whitely was innocent in all of this and her anger should stay directed towards Richard only.

'He went for a ride. I think he was heading towards the lake. Sometimes he swims when the weather is as hot as today.'

'Of course he does,' she muttered, flinging the pile of dresses and fabric onto a chair. 'Point me in the right direction.'

'That way, miss,' Whitely said, directing her with

his finger past the formal gardens and into the parkland beyond.

Hetty grabbed her bonnet, jammed it on her head but did not pause to tie the ribbons. As she strode through the grounds it was quite satisfying to have the fabric flying behind her as if she were a warrior queen of old, allowing her locks to fly free.

She expected some of her anger to have dissipated by the time she reached the lake, but the walk only riled her up even more. *How dare he?* To arrange for the modiste to visit to provide her with a couple of new dresses was a kind gesture, one she was thankful for, despite feeling a little uncomfortable at the generosity of it. The appointment had started well, with the modiste chattering away whilst she took Hetty's measurements, complimenting her on her slim figure. Hetty grimaced—she was not naturally slender in build. Years earlier, she'd had curves, but many years of hard living meant all excess weight had melted from her and left her without the curve of buttocks and breasts she had once had. Still, the modiste had been complimentary and they had moved on to discuss fabrics.

There had been the first point of contention. The modiste had brought a couple of readymade dresses that would need only a few adjustments to fit Hetty, and also rolls and swatches of fabric for Hetty to peruse and admire. Both the dresses and the fabric were beautiful, delicate, expensive, and not at all what Hetty needed. A new dress was a luxury, but it needed to be practical as well, with hard-wearing material and a dark colour to hide all manner of spills and messes. The modiste had eyed Hetty oddly but had acquiesced, describing some plainer material at the shop she could use.

Hetty blew out a sharp breath as she reached the edge of the lake. It was a sweltering day and her fast march through the gardens and the heavy material of her borrowed dress meant she felt uncomfortable in the heat and the glistening water looked inviting. And there was Richard, swimming as if he were king of the lake.

At first, he didn't see her, intent as he was on his swim. He moved rhythmically, propelling himself rapidly through the water. It was only when he reached the far side and turned back that he noticed her standing there.

He swam back quickly, concern etched on his face as he drew closer. 'Is something amiss? Is Noah hurt?'

'Noah is fine.'

Hetty's eyes widened as he reached the shallows and stood. His top half was completely bare, the water lapping at his waist. She felt her eyes drift down, needing to know if he was completely naked under the cover of the water.

'I need to speak to you,' she said, trying to retain the anger she had felt on marching out of the drawing room.

'Might I be allowed to get out of the water first? Or shall we shout at each other like a fisherman and his wife bringing in the catch?'

Hetty pressed her lips together. 'You may get out.' She crossed her arms and waited.

Richard raised an eyebrow, looking down at his naked torso, and then shrugged. 'I suppose you have seen it all before.'

He took a step forward, the water lapping at his waist, and Hetty let out a little cry of frustration before spinning round.

It seemed to take him an age to get out of the water and pull on his breeches, and Hetty's rebellious mind could not help but picture every single second of it. Richard had always been muscular and toned. Hours spent on horseback were partially responsible, but he was also a man who could never sit still. He loved to read, but apart from that all his hobbies and pastimes were active ones.

Hetty tried to dismiss the picture she had of him, but it was impossible. The memory of their first time together would always be etched in her mind. They had been walking by the Douro River, Richard's first foray out into the world when his leg was healed well enough to allow him a little exercise. The sun had been low in the sky and the water shimmered beside them. The rolling hills of Portugal had come alive in the early evening light, the greens and yellows making it look like something out of a painting.

They had found a spot beneath an almond tree and in that moment Hetty had been happier than she'd thought possible. There had been no need to rush, no one waiting for them, and as the sun dipped lower in the sky they had made love for the first time.

'You can turn around,' Richard said, his voice cutting through her memories.

She turned and felt her eyes flick over his body. He was dressed, thankfully, but it hardly made any difference. His clothes were sticking to his body, the thin material of his shirt clinging to the muscles of his chest. As always, his shirtsleeves were rolled up to reveal tanned forearms and Hetty had a flash of memory of how it felt having hold her.

'What was it you wanted to talk to me about?'

Hetty forced herself to look away and compose herself before speaking. 'The modiste is here.'

'Good,' he said, a note of wariness in his voice.

'What did you tell her?'

'The modiste?'

'Yes, the modiste,' Hetty said, momentarily distracted as Richard raised an arm and ran it through his wet hair. He'd always kept it cropped short, citing the hot weather on the Continent and the difficulty in keeping longer hair clean when he was in the army. Now she wondered if it was habit that made him eschew the more fashionable longer styles, or if he knew it made him look even more attractive.

'I can't recall exactly. I sent a note asking her to call upon you at Farnleigh Hall, and that you were desperately in need of some dresses.' He frowned. 'What is this about, Hetty? Not that flea-ridden dress I had burned again?'

'No. It is not about that.'

'Then what? I swear you are the hardest woman to do something nice for.' There was a harder note to his voice now and she was glad of it. It was difficult to be angry with Richard because most of the time he was so reasonable. At least now she could argue with him properly.

'The modiste was most preoccupied with my trousseau, and in particular with the nightgowns and intimate items I might need.'

Richard looked at her in disbelief.

'You're angry at me because the modiste asked you about a trousseau?'

Hetty drew herself up to her full height, which

was still a good few inches shorter than Richard. 'We are not getting married.'

The colour drained from his face and he pressed his lips together. She could see anger flaring in his eyes and wondered if he would let it out or barricade it inside.

'I know we are not getting married, Mrs Fairweather,' he said, almost spitting her name at her. 'Do you know how I know that? Because I have not asked you.'

'But you assumed...'

He laughed mirthlessly. '*I* assumed nothing. I haven't had a chance to assume. Ever since you arrived here you have made it perfectly clear that you no longer wish to share anything apart from our son. You even insist on this stupid formality with names.' He stepped closer so their bodies were only inches apart. 'I know every single inch of your body. I probably know it better than you do yourself. I can tell where each and every freckle is situated, the size of the dimples at the bottom of your back, I could even sketch what is between your legs, yet I must call you *Mrs Fairweather*.'

Hetty was a little taken aback by the passion with which he spoke. She had expected him to explain, perhaps apologise, but not this.

'Three years ago, I would have laid down my life

for you. I was ready to marry you and I would have spent my life worshipping you.' He shook his head, his eyes flicking between her eyes and her lips. 'All I did wrong was assume you were dead when you were lying unmoving, surrounded by the slaughtered. Nothing more. Yet you shy away from me as if I am a monster.'

Hetty shook her head. Surely he had to know it wasn't him she was shying away from.

'The modiste…' she began.

'The modiste has made some assumptions about the nature of our relationship. I cannot be held responsible for that. I told her nothing of you, just that a guest staying at Farnleigh Hall was in need of some new clothes. The sensible thing would have been to gently set her right and then think no more of it, yet here you are angry at me for something I haven't done.'

Feeling the anger inside her deflate, she clenched her fists to stop them from shaking. Richard hadn't moved yet their bodies were even closer and she could feel heat emanating from him.

'I know you do not care for me as once you did,' he said, his voice low now. 'I will not deny that hurt, but I am a grown man, I will survive. What I cannot endure is your constant suspicion. I am not here to hurt you. I am not planning on stealing Noah away from you and I do not mean to ravish you at the first opportunity. The only person jeopardising your future here is you.'

Some of the anger had gone from his voice now, but she could see that she had hurt him. Of course it had been the modiste's mistake. Now she stopped to think about it, that made more sense than Richard going around secretly telling people they were going to be wed. She felt a fool.

She looked up at him and for a moment was lost in his eyes. She wished more than anything that they could erase the last three years and be transported back to the time when everything had seemed so straightforward.

Richard went to turn away, no doubt frustrated with her and the constant drama she was bringing into his life. Instinctively, Hetty reached out and grabbed his wet shirt, stopping him from moving away from her. As she looked up at him she felt something inside her shift a little and she remembered how it felt to be held by this man. She wanted that, the safety, the security, the love, but she knew there was something inside her that would not allow her to accept it.

She cleared her throat, conscious that she was holding him there, unable to think of the words to say to make him understand everything she was feeling.

'I'm sorry,' she managed eventually. 'As I told you before, I am not used to kindness, not without an ulterior motive.' She swallowed, feeling the intensity of his gaze on her. 'When I stop to think about it, I know you would not go about implying to people we were to be married. Of course it is ridiculous.'

She searched his face for a sign that he might forgive her. Still his brow was furrowed and she knew her accusations had wounded him deeply. Without thinking, she reached out and smoothed the lines between his eyes, only realising how intimate her action was when she heard Richard inhale sharply.

'Forgive me, I overstepped,' she said, her hand falling away, but Richard's fingers came up and grabbed it before it reached her side.

For a long moment they stood like that, face to face, with Richard holding her hand in his. Hetty's thoughts were jumbled, she couldn't think straight, and there was a little voice inside her telling her to forget the years of heartache and hurt, to throw her arms around Richard and kiss the man.

Of course she did not move. One voice in her subconscious could not overcome all the pain and all the doubts that had been laid on top of it.

Eventually, it was Richard who moved away. He strode over to where he had left his clothes and picked up his jacket.

'I know we cannot go back to how we were, Hetty,' he said quietly, his back still turned away from her. 'And I think perhaps that is for the best, but it does not mean I wish you anything but happiness. May I suggest that we focus on learning how to live alongside one another these next few weeks? I plan to be part of Noah's life and, as such, whatever you think of me, you are stuck with me. But that does not mean there has to be any suspicion or animosity. I promise to think of you as nothing more than Noah's mother. How does that sound?'

There was a formality in his voice that she knew she had forced there and for an instant she hated herself and her impulsiveness.

'That sounds like a very sensible idea,' she said.

'Good. Tomorrow we will visit the injured man together and next week I plan to host a dinner.' He held up a hand to quieten any protest. 'I think it is necessary. There will be rumours in the local area that I have a woman and her child staying with me. If we let the gossip run unchecked, everyone will assume the worst. By inviting a few select guests we can spin the tale that you are an impoverished relative who has fallen on hard times and sought sanctuary here at Farnleigh Hall.'

Hetty nodded. When he put it like that, there was nothing to argue with.

'No one will know who you really are, apart from my dear friend Major Redfern. He remembers you from our time on the Peninsular.'

'You trust him, I presume.'

'With my life.'

'Then we have nothing to fear from him.'

'No.' Richard took hold of his horse's reins, a different animal to the horse he had ridden two days earlier, and began to lead him back towards the house. 'I hope you managed to finalise the details of which dresses the modiste will make for you before you stormed all the way across the grounds.'

Hetty felt the colour rise in her cheeks. 'I did, although I may need to apologise for my abrupt departure.'

'Perhaps we can call at her shop on the way through Bamburgh tomorrow.'

'I would like to make another stop in Bamburgh too. There was a carriage accident on our journey here and a little girl was injured.'

'That *was* you,' Richard murmured, then shook his head. 'I saw you in the back of the cart as it disappeared around the corner. At the time I dismissed the sighting as a trick my mind played on me.' He nodded. 'Very well, we will stop in Bamburgh on our way.'

'Thank you,' she said, falling into step beside him.

Chapter Eight

Richard turned over another page of figures written in his steward's neat hand and rubbed his brow. The journey to Bamburgh took a little over half an hour in the carriage and he had thought it a good time to go through some of the accounts he had been neglecting for too long. He did not often use the carriage, he much preferred to be out in the open on horseback, even if the weather wasn't agreeable, but he knew not many people shared his preference. Hetty was one who clearly preferred the carriage to horseback, and today she was sitting across from him, assiduously avoiding his gaze.

She was a woman of many talents, and keeping calm under pressure was one of them. He'd witnessed her suturing wounds whilst a battle raged only a few hundred feet away, seemingly oblivious. That was why her outburst yesterday had seemed so out of character. Even if she felt he had done something wrong he would have expected her to come to him with a well-reasoned argument, not storm across half the estate looking for him in anger.

Perhaps it showed how little he really knew her. Or perhaps it was a sign of how much she had changed these last few years.

One day, when she had settled in, he would ask her more about the time she had spent without him, the three years when she'd had to return to her husband with an illegitimate child. She had hinted that they had been difficult years, and he was not surprised. Hetty had told him a little of her husband and how he had treated her when they were together in Cidade Velha do Douro, and he had also heard accounts of the man from fellow officers. The army was vast but bad apples stood out and were noted, and Phillip Fairweather had been one of them.

He was thankful when the carriage slowed as they reached Bamburgh. It was a small settlement, not much more than a high street and a few roads beyond, but for the rural community of this part of Northumberland it was the hub of all activity. There were a number of shops dotted along the high street as well as an apothecary and the house of the local doctor. A church stood a little way back from the main street, but it was the castle that held the dominating position over the town.

'That is quite a fortress,' Hetty said, looking up at it in awe.

'It is still inhabited,' Richard said.

'Noah would love it. He adores playing knights and villains, or knights and dragons, or knights and anything.'

'The family who reside there are quite private, but there is another castle a little further down the coast, Dunstanburgh Castle. It is a ruin, open to the elements, but it is heaven for a young boy to explore. I went there a few times with my brothers and we played for hours in the half tumbledown towers and underground rooms.'

'Is it safe?'

'It is on the edge of a cliff so I would not let Noah explore unsupervised, but the castle has been standing in its current condition for a long time. I do not think it will fall any time soon.'

Hetty gave him a small smile, acknowledging the effort he was making to ensure normality between them after their argument the day before. 'Then perhaps we might make a trip of it one day.'

The carriage rolled to a stop and Richard hopped down, turning back to assist Hetty. The touch of her hand was fleeting but he felt the pleasing warmth of her skin as her fingers touched his.

'Where first? The modiste or to see your patient?'

'The modiste's shop is on the way, let us pop in there first.' Hetty paused. 'I am aware these are my errands to run. If you wish to stay in the carriage and continue with your paperwork I will not be offended.'

'Good Lord, there is nothing I would like less. I have strong feelings about the accounts and they are not positive ones.'

'Surely your steward does most of the work.'

'Are you trying to make me feel even worse?' he said with a grimace. 'Evans does practically everything. All I need to do is check things over and leave a note with any discrepancies or ideas I have. The man is a saint, and a very talented land steward, yet I still find it tiresome to do my part of the work.'

'You never shied away from the difficult when you were in the army.'

'The difficult didn't include column after column of incomings and outgoings.'

Hetty frowned. 'With your expensive education, that should not be an issue.'

'It shouldn't. I never found arithmetic or reasoning difficult at school.'

With her head tilted to the side, she regarded him, stopping in the middle of the pavement to consider this snippet of information. 'You know why you find it so difficult, don't you?'

He shrugged.

'You do, or at least you think you do.'

Richard took her arm and moved her to the side of the pavement so she wasn't in anyone's way.

'It doesn't matter. I employ an exemplary steward so I do not need to worry too much.'

'It is because you feel you do not deserve it, that the estate should not be yours.'

'But it is mine,' he said, his voice low. 'My responsibility, therefore my work. Your reasoning does not stand up to scrutiny.'

'Not when you think about it logically, but our minds are completely *illogical*. Somewhere deep inside, you feel as if you have stolen what should have been your brother's and it means you cannot do what is needed for the estate.'

'I hardly think I am that easily fooled by my own brain,' he objected, even though he was aware that in a few short seconds Hetty had got to the crux of the matter. He was perfectly capable of reading through the accounts and making decisions about the estate but he procrastinated, not from disinterest but from a sense that it shouldn't be his to make decisions about.

'Hmm,' she said before he quickly ushered her in to the modiste.

'Mrs Fairweather, how delightful to see you again

so soon!' Mrs Taylor said as she hurried out from behind her counter. 'And it is always a pleasure, Lord Westbridge.'

She dipped down into a polite curtsey that Richard acknowledged with a nod. He always felt a little ridiculous when the locals treated him with such deference. In the army he had been a staunch advocate of good discipline and the importance of observance of rank; in an organisation of that size it was vital that everyone knew their place and there were consequences for stepping out of it. Yet here, in the sleepy village of Bamburgh, it felt unnecessary.

Hetty looked around her, ensuring there were no other customers close by, and then leaned in towards Mrs Taylor.

'I wanted to apologise for leaving so abruptly yesterday.'

'I am sorry if I offended you with questions about your trousseau,' Mrs Taylor said, wringing her hands.

'Your questions were not said in malice,' Hetty replied quietly, 'I know that. It is just that I am recently widowed and I find certain things upset me even when they should not.'

'My deepest sympathy, Mrs Fairweather, but please do not worry yourself, we will speak no more of it. Now, I have one of your dresses almost ready if you would like to see it. Not one of the custom-made pieces, but one that I have altered.'

Hetty disappeared into the back section of the shop with the dressmaker and Richard took a seat, reclining on one of the comfortable chairs set out for those waiting. He didn't expect Hetty to reappear, so when Mrs Taylor ushered her out he sprang to his feet in surprise.

The dress was simple in cut and material but well crafted, and highlighted Hetty's attributes perfectly. It was light blue in colour, with a white ribbon sash just under the bust and the skirt cut straight to accentuate her height and slenderness.

'What do you think?' Hetty asked, biting her lip. He could see she was pleased with the dress and he chose his words carefully, knowing she would not want him to be overly enthusiastic but needing gentle words of encouragement.

'It suits you very well,' he said with a soft smile. 'The colour is perfect on you and it looks as if it were made for you—it fits very well.'

'I do not know how you have worked your magic so quickly,' Hetty said to Mrs Taylor. The older woman's cheeks flushed and she had a look of satisfaction on her face.

'The dress was almost finished. I just needed to

alter one or two things once I had your measurements.'

'I love it, Mrs Taylor.'

'Would you like to wear it now? Or shall I pack it for you?'

Hetty bit her lip, clearly unused to having something made just for her.

'She'll wear it now,' he said decisively. 'Perhaps you would be so kind as to pack the dress she came in.'

Mrs Taylor bustled around for a few minutes, making the final adjustments to Hetty's dress and packing the old one, and then they were out of the shop and back on the street.

Before they moved away from the dressmaker's shop Hetty caught his arm. 'Thank you,' she said, holding his gaze. 'I know this dress has been a point of contention between us, but I do appreciate what you have done for me.'

'You're welcome,' he said with a shrug. 'It is only a dress.'

'No, it isn't. It is a gesture of generosity.'

He frowned, not quite understanding.

'When I was reunited with Phillip he was bitter about the life I had led without him, quite happily, when he disappeared. He was dishonourably discharged from the army for his desertion and in a foul temper when we returned to England.' Hetty slipped her arm through his and continued talking as they walked. She had let a few things slip about her late husband this last week, but it was heartening that she felt able to properly open up to him, as if she was gradually becoming more comfortable with him. 'Back home, he would find work for a short period of time but then drink himself into a stupor and lose the job quickly. Money was tight, until I realised I needed to be the one to support us. I let it be known I had picked up some nursing skills in Portugal and before long I had a steady stream of people wanting my services. The local doctor was supportive—if someone needed a little extra help whilst they recovered, he would put them in contact with me.'

'You were the one who supported your family?'

'I couldn't rely on Phillip. Even when it was my money coming into the household I did not have control of it. I would squirrel away just enough for the rent and to cover food for the week, but he would have the rest.' She paused and glanced up at him, giving a little self-aware smile. 'Here is where the story becomes relevant. I only had two dresses. They were both old, shabby and mended many times over. One started to fall apart in ways that could not be mended, and I asked Phillip for the money to buy a new one. Nothing fancy, just a basic brown work dress. We could just about afford it, but he said no, and spent the money on liquor instead.'

'I'm sorry.'

'So you see it is important, and it is kind of you. I know you are wealthy, but it is still generous to think of me when even my own husband would not.'

'That is why you only had the one dress when you arrived at Farnleigh Hall?'

Hetty grimaced. 'Partly, but once my husband had died his family swept in and took everything. Even though most of the things we owned had been bought with the money I had earned.'

'They disliked you so much?'

'He spun a story of him being injured in battle and me leaving him behind to have my dalliance with a senior officer. He was the beloved son and brother and I was the woman who had given birth to another man's child.'

'At least you are free of them all now.'

Hetty paused and then looked up at him. 'You're right. I am free. Free of Phillip and free of his horrible family. I never have to see them again.'

There was a lightness about her step after this and Richard had to wonder how awful Hetty's life had been these last three years.

'Here we are,' he said as they stopped outside a

door in the poorer part of the village. It was a little terraced cottage, the garden nicely kept, but needing a coat of paint around the windows.

She knocked and the door was opened by a thin woman who looked pale and drawn, although her face lit up when she saw Hetty.

'Mrs Fairweather, it is so good of you to call!'

'I wanted to see how Rose fared.'

'She is doing well, thanks to you. Although she is melancholy that she cannot go out and play with her friends in this glorious weather we've been having.' The woman's eyes slipped to Richard and then a panicked look crossed her face. 'Lord Westbridge?'

'I am sorry to intrude,' he said, wondering if his reputation was so fearful amongst the local people.

'I am staying with Lord Westbridge at present, he is a distant relative,' Hetty said, spinning the lie they had agreed on.

'It is an honour, my lord. If I had known you were coming…' The woman trailed off as she looked behind her into her humble home.

'I do not wish to put you to any inconvenience,' Richard said, hating that he might make the woman feel uncomfortable.

'It is no intrusion, my lord. It is an honour.' She ushered them both inside. The cottage was small but clean and tidy and it looked like a well-loved family home.

'Rose is in here. We were not able to get her up the stairs with her leg so my husband brought her bed down in the parlour.'

'Has the doctor visited again?' Hetty asked, beaming as she saw the little girl she had helped a week earlier.

'No,' the woman said quietly. 'We cannot afford a second visit, so we just have to hope he set the leg right the first time. Rose has been ever so good and has made every effort not to move it from its bindings.'

Richard watched as Hetty knelt down beside the girl's bed and took her hand.

'It is good to see you, Rose.'

'And you too, Mrs Fairweather.'

'How do you fare?'

'My leg hurts a little less each day but Mama says I will have to stay in bed for another five weeks!' She pulled a face at the prospect.

'I know it is a bore, but a broken leg is no small injury. We want you to be able to walk on that leg again, and that means resting it for now.'

Richard smiled at Hetty's kind but firm tone as it transported him back to the makeshift hospital in Cidade Velha do Douro. The soldiers there who had been her patients had obeyed her without question, and it would seem she had not lost her skills of persuasion.

'I wanted to ask you about afterwards,' Rose's mother said, a note of anxiety in her voice. 'Surely the strength in her legs will have wasted away, where she is in bed all day and all night.'

'Yes,' Hetty said, choosing to tell the truth even though it wasn't what the mother wanted to hear. 'The recovery for a broken bone should be thought of as twelve weeks. Six of keeping as still as possible in bed, without any stress to the bone whilst it heals. Then six to gradually get back on her feet. Rose will have to work hard to regain her strength, but it is possible. I have seen men with much worse injuries return to full function within a few months.'

'There, you hear that, Rose—it'll be hard work but you'll be running around the village again with your friends by the autumn.'

'What do you do to amuse yourself, Rose?' Richard asked, spying a book at her bedside. He knew of the Miller family. The father worked as a farrier, and Richard would not expect the girls of the family to be taught to read.

'I read, my lord,' she said, indicating the book by her bed. 'Although I've read this one twice this week already as there is so little else to do.'

'May I?' he said, indicating the book.

Rose nodded, hugging her rag doll to her.

'*The Adventures of Miss Thornlax*,' he read. 'It is not one I know.'

'Miss Elm, the local schoolteacher, lent it to her,' Mrs Miller said by way of explanation.

'You go to school, Rose?'

'Yes, my lord. I love school and I particularly love Miss Elm.'

'You must be missing it.'

Rose nodded.

'We send all our children to school, my lord. My husband says an education is the way to a better future.'

'I agree with your husband, Mrs Miller, and I must commend you on your efforts. I know education is not cheap, especially when you have more than one child.'

'Rose is one of four, our only girl, but she has ambitions to be a schoolteacher herself when she is older.'

'You will need that education then, Rose,' Richard said with a smile. 'Forgive me if I overstep, but I have a vast library that does not get enough use. I would be happy to send over some books to keep you amused whilst you recuperate, if you would like.'

Rose's eyes lit up but Richard hardly noticed. All he saw was how Hetty beamed up at him.

'Mrs Fairweather, I might need your assistance in choosing something suitable,' Richard said.

'Of course,' Hetty said, 'We shall search as soon as we return to Farnleigh Hall and choose a half dozen to keep you occupied these next few weeks.'

'You are too kind, my lord,' Mrs Miller said, her voice cracking with emotion.

'I remember the boredom of being trapped in a bed with an injury far too well. The days all blur into one unless you have something to focus on.' He glanced at Hetty and saw she understood his meaning. His shining light had been Hetty. She had got him through his convalescence. Every day he had waited for her to hurry into the church, her face lit with a smile, always happy to give her time and companionship.

Richard stepped back whilst Hetty checked the girl over, making sure the splint on her leg was still secure. He wondered if perhaps they might get back to that happy companionship again one day. In Portugal it had been the basis for them falling in love, but perhaps even without a romantic relationship they might share a friendship.

He wondered if he could be content with that, and realised he could. *That* was what he should work towards. A friendship with Hetty and a loving relationship with his son. It might be difficult, he would have to learn to ignore the way his heart thumped in his chest every time she smiled at him, and how his body yearned for her when he caught a hint of her scent, but most difficulties in life could be overcome with a little patience and perseverance.

Once Hetty was satisfied with her young patient they said their farewells and headed for the door.

At the threshold Mrs Miller grasped Hetty by the hand and beamed at her. 'Thank you so much for everything. The doctor said if you hadn't splinted her leg for the journey back home it could have been much worse.'

'I'm just glad I could help.'

Chapter Nine

They were back in the carriage, travelling a little further up the coast to see the man Richard had asked for her assistance with. Hetty felt contented, and as she looked out of the window she could not help the smile that spread across her lips.

'I realise I cannot profess to know you well any longer,' Richard said, the pile of papers next to him untouched for this short journey. 'But I think this is the role that suits you the best.'

'How do you mean?'

'You shine when you help people. You did when you were in Portugal and you do now, here in England.'

'I do like being useful.'

'And you are good at it.'

'Even when life seemed difficult these last few years, I found pleasure in helping people.'

'You should listen to that, find a way to incorporate it into your future.'

Hetty bit her lip. She could not imagine her future right now. At the moment she was still living in a bit of a daze. Every morning when she woke up she felt that surge of panic, as she had before Phillip had died. The burden of another day spent wondering what cruelty he might attempt next. It took a few minutes of deep breathing, of telling herself that life was different now, that Phillip could not hurt her any more, before she could believe that that part of her life was over.

'I cannot imagine what the future might hold,' she said quietly.

It was something that was difficult to admit. Once, a long time ago, her head had been filled with dreams. She'd come from a modest family, but had received a decent education and had hoped to better her position in the world. That had been when her mother was alive—a woman who had been full of joie de vivre and encouragement for her young daughter. After her mother's death, everything had unravelled. Her father had started drinking, and Hetty had looked for a way out of the uncomfortable home that she had once loved so much. She'd thought Phillip was the answer, hoped he was her knight in shining armour, and as such she had ignored the voice of doubt inside her.

Now she had Noah, the most important person in the world, someone to strive for, to prove herself for, yet she had lost sight of her own dreams.

'You will,' Richard said with his customary confidence.

She appreciated his faith in her, but she wasn't sure. For years her wants and desires had been suppressed. Maybe it was difficult to let them to the surface again.

Before she could say any more the carriage slowed. They were in the middle of nowhere, pulled to the side of the road with no houses in sight.

'I can't get any closer with the carriage, my lord,' the groom said as he hopped down and came to the carriage window. 'You'll have to go the rest of the way on foot.'

As they alighted Hetty saw a small dwelling in the distance. It was set at one end of a small cove, just back from the sand. From here it hardly looked like a house at all, more like a fishing shack or a shelter for boats, but she knew there were all sorts of homes that people were forced to live in. In her home county of Essex, alongside the quaint villages with pretty cottages were people living in such poverty it was painful to see them emerge from homes not even fit for animals.

They walked in silence, picking their way over the rocks until there was sand under their feet, Hetty careful to hold the hem of her new dress high enough so it would not soak up the water from the beach.

'So you have never met this man before?' Hetty asked as they approached the cottage.

'No. Major Redfern brought him to my attention and arranged our visit here today. He is a man of many contacts and keeps up with his old connections from the army. If he hears of someone injured and needing help, he lets me know.'

'Like your footman, Whitely?'

'Exactly, although I knew Whitely myself. He was one of the young lads under my command for a short while. Poor boy was only in the army three months before he took a bullet to the leg. He was discharged and struggled to find work, even though he is strong and clever and honest.'

'There are a lot of able-bodied men looking for work. I suppose many people do not want to take a risk on a man who might not be able to do as many of the physical tasks.'

'I expect you're right. People are fools—on the whole, ex-soldiers are disciplined and hard workers. Even with an injury they will often do more work than an able-bodied man,' Richard said, cutting off the conversation abruptly as he rapped on the door of the shack.

The door opened after a minute and a young woman with a toddler on her hip looked out. She was painfully thin, her cheekbones protruding and her eyes sunken and a layer of grime about her that indicated she had not bathed for quite some time.

For a moment she looked up at them, seeming not to understand that she had visitors at her door.

'Good morning, Mrs Brent. I am Lord Westbridge and this is Mrs Fairweather. We have come to enquire about your husband. I think Major Redfern may have informed you of our visit.'

'Yes,' she said and then dipped into a shaky curtsey. 'Come in.'

Hetty hesitated at the doorway and then leaned in to Richard. 'We should send your groom for milk and bread. That will help this family more than anything else.'

She followed Mrs Brent into the dark house, steeling herself as the smell hit. There was the underlying stench of decay, as if the ancient wooden planks that made up the shack's exterior walls were slowly rotting from the inside out. Then there was a sharper, more noticeable smell of the sea and Hetty saw the nets hanging up on one wall. No doubt before his stint in the navy Mr Brent had been a fisherman, but the nets now hung unused and slowly falling apart on the wall.

There was only one room, so once inside it was difficult to miss Mr Brent's supine form, even in the darkness.

'Would you like something to drink?' The woman cast around as if looking for something she could give her guests.

'No, thank you,' Richard said quickly. He made his way over to Mr Brent, who was wincing as he pushed himself up in the bed. 'I am Lord Westbridge, it is good to meet you.'

'You're an army man?' Mr Brent said, his voice raspy.

'Yes. Although not in active service any longer. I fought on the Peninsular.'

Richard pulled up a chair and sat down next to the man and Hetty marvelled at how easily he slipped into this role. Perhaps it came from his time in the army—as a commander of men he had been privy to their private business, both salubrious and less so. He had never held himself apart like so many of the other officers, and it meant that men like Mr Brent found it easy to trust him.

'I've brought Mrs Fairweather with me. She is a nurse and dealt with many injured men in Portugal.

She has seen everything, and is skilled at what she does. I wonder if you would permit her to examine you, perhaps help with your dressings.'

'It will not be a pleasant sight,' Mr Brent said.

'I will give you some privacy whilst she works. I wonder, Mrs Brent, if there is somewhere to get clean water close by?'

'There is a well out back.' She made to go and fetch it.

'Please, permit me,' he said, motioning for her to stay where she was. 'I also need to speak to my groom so I will be back in a few minutes.'

'Good morning,' Hetty said as she approached the man in the bed. In the years she had been doing work such as this she had become immune to the sights and smells that she could be confronted with. Once she had been asked to see to a man's leg that had a great ulcer upon it. The stench had been almost unbearable, but the worst thing was the dozens of maggots crawling about the wound. 'I wonder if you could tell me a little about your injuries before I start.'

'I was burned when the *HMS Forthright* caught fire. I was down below and there was no way out until the deck had burned all the way through. I then managed to escape up a ladder and dive off into the sea.'

'The navy doctors treated your wounds?'

He scoffed. 'They gave me laudanum because they thought I would die, and then they left me screaming in pain for three days straight.'

'I am sorry to hear it. I have not seen every type of injury, of course, but I think burns are the absolute worst.'

'He was sent home with his flesh still raw,' Mrs Brent said, high emotion in her voice.

'Where are the burns, Mr Brent?'

'All over the left side of my body. From neck to ankle.'

'Your face was spared.'

'More or less.'

'How about your hands?'

'The left is burned, that is perhaps the most painful part.'

'And have you seen a doctor since you arrived back home?'

'No. We have no money for it. Not with a wife and child to support and no income.' Mr Brent spoke quietly. He was only a young man, perhaps twenty-two or twenty-three. He should have his whole life stretching out before him, fathering more children, earning money to support his family. Instead, the navy had chewed him up and spat him out, a shell of the man he had been when he'd gone in.

'Who changes your dressings?'

'My wife helps me to bathe, but no one has changed the dressings in weeks.'

Hetty swallowed hard. Burns were notoriously hard to care for. They often became infected and the large area they could cover meant they were slow to heal.

'Do you mind if I have a look? It may hurt.'

'Pain is my constant companion.'

'I am sure it is,' Hetty murmured. She looked over her shoulder to where Mrs Brent had slumped into a chair, the toddler sitting quietly on her lap. This was a family on the brink of complete collapse. If something were not done, then she would wager they would all be dead within a month.

Carefully, she pulled back the blanket that covered Mr Brent and began to inspect the wounds. He had some filthy bandages wound around much of it and as she carefully tried to lift these away he howled in pain.

'Forgive me,' she said, resting back on her haunches. After two more attempts she stopped, pulled the blanket back over him and stood up.

'I will be back in a moment,' she said, smiling her most reassuring smile and stepping out of the shack.

Hetty sucked in great breaths, trying to stem the tears that threatened to fall down her cheeks. The world suddenly felt very unfair. No doubt Mr Brent had enlisted hoping the regular pay from the navy would give his young family a better life. Now they were destitute, with no hope of being saved.

'How bad is it?' Richard murmured as he came from the back of the house carrying a bucket of water.

'Bad.'

'Is there anything you can do?'

'Here? No.' She shook her head to emphasise her point. 'The house is too filthy. He has nothing to numb the pain. He is malnourished and hours away from an infection that will kill him.'

'And elsewhere?'

She frowned, not understanding his meaning.

'If he were taken somewhere clean with good food and adequate medicine, with access to clean water and clean dressings, would he have a chance?'

She thought for a moment. 'Perhaps a one in five chance of surviving.' She grimaced, knowing the odds were completely against Mr Brent.

'One in five,' Richard mused. 'That is not nothing. Come, let us go talk to the Brents. Richardson, my groom, has gone to buy bread and milk and a little cheese and meat for the family. We have a few minutes.'

Hetty caught his arm. 'He knows he is dying.'

Richard did not shrug her off, just gave her a half smile, half grimace. 'Sometimes the only thing we can do is keep fighting.'

It felt even darker and smaller when they were back inside the house and Hetty initially stood back whilst Richard arranged the chair so that he and Hetty as well as Mrs Brent could sit around Mr Brent's bed.

'I am sorry for your injuries,' Richard began, 'and for the way the navy has treated you. None of that I can change.'

'I thank you for your sympathy, but none of it is your fault.' Mr Brent winced as he shifted in the bed.

'I think you are dying, Mr Brent. Slowly and painfully.'

Hetty heard herself gasp at his bluntness, but Mr Brent only nodded sagely.

'Yes, I am.'

'Your wounds are extensive but, more than that, you and your family are starving.'

'Lord Westbridge,' Hetty said, a warning tone in her voice. She was in favour of honesty, but there were ways of discussing important matters without this bluntness.

'No, let him be, Mrs Fairweather. The Earl is only speaking plain.'

'You have no family, no one to support you or your wife?'

'No. No one. When I am gone, Lizzie and Tom will be all alone.'

Richard paused, looking the man over. 'I can give you food, a promise to ensure your wife and your son will be taken care of when you die.'

Mr Brent reached out and took Richard's hand and gripped it so tightly that Hetty could see the injured man wince in pain at the effort.

'If you would do that then I could die happy.'

'You may not need to die, Mr Brent.' Richard paused and glanced at Hetty. 'I cannot guarantee your survival, but I can offer you the option of a chance.'

'I don't understand. My wounds…'

'Are severe, I agree. Yet men have survived worse and gone on to live full and functional lives.' Richard spoke quickly now, sensing both hope and disbelief from the young couple. 'If you stay here you will die. What I propose is to move you to a house where you can recover. It is clean and dry and has plentiful food. There would be visits from a doctor and, if Mrs Fairweather would be kind enough to assist, someone very capable dressing your wounds.'

Mr Brent stared at him as if he were mad. 'We don't have the funds to pay for any of that, my lord.'

'I do.'

'Why would you do that for me? For us?'

'I cannot help every poor soul in this world, but I can help some of them.' He shrugged. 'I know the strain of time spent in service to the country. I also know a little of what it is like to be injured, to have your life change for ever. I want to help you, Mr Brent, but it is your choice as to whether you wish to accept that help.'

'I would be a fool not to.'

'I do not promise it to be without its difficulties.'

'There might be a significant amount of pain, and you may still not survive,' Hetty said gently.

'I don't care. If there is a chance…' He reached out and took his wife's hand.

'Then I will make the arrangements. My groom will be returning with a little food, but can I suggest we put this plan into action as soon as possible? I will arrange for a carriage and cart to collect you and your belongings tomorrow.'

Richard stood and Hetty followed him as he headed towards the door.

'Thank you,' Mrs Brent said quietly, 'for giving us a chance.'

When they were outside Hetty felt the emotion of the last few minutes wash over her. She had stood outside only ten minutes earlier, convinced Mr Brent would die in the coming weeks and his family would follow soon after without him to provide for them. Now he had a chance, however small.

She looked up at Richard, who was watching for the groom making his way across the sand as if he hadn't just saved three lives.

'That is the kindest act I have ever witnessed.'

Richard shook his head. 'I have money—far too much money for one man. What sort of person would I be if I spent it all on myself rather than giving those who fought alongside me at least a chance in this world?'

This was not her family, but she did feel a strange sort of elation, mixed in with sorrow at the state that they had been reduced to.

As they headed back over the sands towards the carriage, Hetty's hand brushed accidentally against Richard's. He did not react, perhaps he did not even notice, it was such an insignificant touch, but she didn't instinctively flinch at the contact. Telling herself not to make a big deal out of it, she walked on, curling her fingers into a loose fist protectively, as if she didn't want to lose the memory of their touch.

Chapter Ten

Hetty awoke suddenly, sitting up in bed in an instant, her senses on high alert. She had fallen asleep hours earlier, after hearing all about Noah's wonderful day with his new nursemaid. Something had woken her, she was sure of it, and at first she thought it might be Noah calling out for her.

Quickly she rose, pulling on her dressing gown over her thin nightgown, and hurried to the nursery. As she poked her head inside she heard Noah's steady deep breathing and saw his sleeping form tucked up under the blanket. He had a stuffed bear tucked into bed with him, a teddy he had found in one of the cupboards of the nursery. Richard had told her it used to be one of his brother's, but had not seemed to mind that Noah had adopted it.

She watched for a moment, satisfying herself that Noah was sleeping peacefully and not in the midst of a bad dream, before heading back to her bedroom.

She was just about to climb back into bed when she heard the noise again. Someone was crying out, shouting in distress, the sound ringing loud through the house for a few seconds before fading away.

Farnleigh Hall was large and housed a huge number of servants, but their rooms were either above hers on the fourth floor or down in the basement. This sounded closer than that.

Hetty made a quick decision and bypassed her door, continuing down the corridor to the staircase. The cry came again, guiding her down, until she was standing outside Richard's room.

She knocked gently, her heart thumping as she wondered if he was injured somehow. It was hard to imagine what could befall a man in the middle of the night in his own home, but accidents did happen. Perhaps he had burned himself on an open flame or fallen and injured a limb.

When there was no response Hetty hesitated for only a second before turning the handle and pushing open the door.

The room was in complete darkness, the curtains drawn shut and letting in no light from the moon. For a moment Hetty couldn't see anything more than a couple of feet in front of her, but slowly her eyes adjusted and she could make out the shapes of the furniture.

The cry came again, so anguished that Hetty rushed forward.

'Lord Westbridge… Richard…what is the matter?'

There was silence, no answer from anywhere in the room.

Deciding she could not assess the situation without a little light, she moved around the edge of the room until she felt the heavy fabric of the curtains in her hands. She flung them open, glad of the moonlight that shone in.

Finally, she could see enough to work out what was happening. Richard was in his bed, naked at least from the waist up. A sheet covered his lower half and his modesty, but for a moment Hetty was transported back to a time when she had lain with her skin pressed against his, revelling in the feel of his taut muscles as he embraced her.

He was asleep, although tossing and turning in his bed as if bewitched. He let out another cry and Hetty felt her heart lurch. Whatever it was he was dreaming of was not pleasant. He sounded in such distress that she knew instinctively he was reliving something terrible from the war.

Slowly she approached the bed, trying to recall all the advice she had ever heard about waking people from nightmares. She knew it was considered dangerous to wake someone who was sleepwalking, but she did not think the same applied to bad dreams. Surely Richard needed saving from whatever terror was visiting him in his sleep.

'Lord Westbridge...' she said, placing a hand gently on his arm.

'No, not the children,' he mumbled, and then let out a strangled cry of frustration and despair.

'Richard, you're dreaming. It's not real,' she said with more force.

'Please...don't do it. Have some humanity...' The words were slurred but she could make out enough to understand their meaning.

'Richard,' she said, louder this time, gripping his arm and shaking him.

She was standing on the right side of the bed, between him and the window, leaning over and slightly off-balance. His arm shot out as he flung himself over, eyes still closed. The force of his arm made her totter and fall forwards, her hands making contact with his chest as her body fought to stay upright.

'Oof!' He let out a sharp exhalation, and in the moonlight Hetty could see his eyes flying open.

For a moment she could not move, surprised by the position she found herself in and unbalanced as she was stretched forwards with her hands on his chest.

'Hetty?'

'You were having a nightmare,' she managed to stutter, aware that it looked as if she was assaulting him in his bed.

He grimaced. 'I was.'

'You were shouting out—I came to see what was the matter.' Still she was bent over him, her hands warm against his skin.

'And you thought you would jump on top of me to wake me?' He raised an eyebrow as he looked down at his naked body with her hands pressed against him.

Hetty cleared her throat and pushed up and away, shaking her hands as she straightened as if she had been burned.

'I fell,' she muttered, feeling the heat from the blood that had rushed to her skin in her embarrassment. 'I'll go.' She spun and was about to flee when Richard's hand shot out and grabbed hold of her wrist. Panic flooded through her and she stiffened, her shoulders hunching as she waited for the blow to come.

'Forgive me,' Richard said gently, dropping her wrist. 'I didn't mean to hurt you.'

'You didn't.'

She hated the way her body responded to a sudden touch, how she was primed to think any rapid movement was a fist flying towards her, ready to cripple her with pain.

'Hetty, please wait.' He pushed himself up in bed, pulling the sheet up to preserve his dignity, although his torso was still bare.

Unbidden, Hetty's eyes flicked to where skin met sheet before she quickly looked away. She found it puzzling how her body could react to him in two such conflicting ways. Part of her wanted to crawl into bed with him, take the comfort and the love he would offer her and surrender to his touch. The other part wanted to flee and curl up in a ball in a locked room so no one could hurt her.

She stopped and turned.

'Come here,' he said, motioning for her to step closer again.

As if in a trance, she moved towards him, stopping only when she was beside his bed.

'Sit down a moment.'

'Richard...'

'On my honour, I will not touch you.'

Hetty perched on the very edge of the bed.

'Surely you must know I would never hurt you?' Richard said.

'I do.'

'I would never force myself on you.'

'I know.'

'Yet you flinch at my touch.'

Hetty's eyes came up to meet his in the moonlight and even in the darkness of the room his blue eyes glinted and sparkled.

'I flinch even sometimes when Noah touches me and I'm not prepared for it,' she said so quietly she was not sure Richard heard her. 'Phillip did not hit me very often but, in a way, I think that was worse. There was always the threat of violence, the knowledge that at some point he would really hurt me.'

'He hit you?' Richard blew out his cheeks and looked at her with such pity that Hetty wished she hadn't told him.

'He did. So, you see, the way I flinch when you touch me is not because it is you I fear, but my body and my mind still respond with fear…'

Richard slowly reached out and touched his fingers to the back of her hand. 'So if I touch you like this then, when it is not unexpected, not threatening…?'

Hetty swallowed. She hadn't realised quite how much she had missed Richard's touch. His gentle caress sent waves of pleasure through her body and for a moment she could think of nothing but his fingers on her skin.

'Then I do not react by lashing out or running away.'

He did not stop, his fingers moving ever so gently backwards and forwards across her skin. Hetty felt heat rise within her, pressing her to take things further, to turn so she was facing Richard fully and to lean in to his embrace.

She closed her eyes, for a moment imagining a world where she could give in to her desires and fall into bed with this man she had loved before. It was an enticing fantasy, one that she knew could never be anything more than a dream. Richard was the best man she had ever known. He was kind and generous and courageous, and he had lost more than one man could bear in a lifetime. He deserved someone who could love him fully, who could lean in to him and return that love. Not a woman scarred by life, who jumped every time he touched her.

She felt a lump forming in her throat. She'd never thought she would ever feel desire again. It was too cruel that when she did, it was for a man she had no right to claim.

'What do you dream about?'

'You do not want to know,' Richard said, his fingers pausing on her skin, a shadow crossing his face.

'You were very distressed.'

'I saw some terrible things in the war, things that have lodged somewhere deep in my brain and worm their way out into my dreams at night-time.'

'I am sorry.'

'It is not your fault.'

Hetty gave a half smile. 'We are a pair, you and I, are we not? Haunted by our ghosts.'

She made the mistake of looking at him again, taking in his shadowed profile in the moonlight. She felt that flare of desire deep inside and found her body swaying forwards, her lips parting ever so slightly. She caught herself, but not before Richard must have seen her intention.

Ever so kindly, as if dealing with a spinster aunt, he spoke. 'I think it is time you returned to your bed, Hetty.'

Inside her something shattered and she was left with a feeling of embarrassment and shame. Quickly, she stood, not meeting his eye, and started for the door. Only when she was at the door did she pause.

'Goodnight, my lord. I hope your sleep is undisturbed by dreams the rest of the night.'

Richard watched Hetty's slender form slip out of his bedroom before collapsing back on his pillows and groaning. Having her here, sitting on his bed, so close yet so far removed from him, had been torture. He'd wanted nothing more than to throw her back onto the pillows and ravish her, to remind her of why they were so compatible, how they had spent hours making love during their short time together in Portugal.

Yet he was a gentleman and her friend. She was fragile, vulnerable, and to take advantage of her would be unforgivable. That was why he'd had to send her away so abruptly. Already his body was taut with desire, thoughts of what he would like to do with her coursing through him. She'd only had to look at him for one more second as if she would like to be kissed and he would have lost control.

'You have been celibate for far too long,' he murmured, flinging an arm back in frustration and grabbing hold of the wooden headboard. He had not touched a woman in three years. Three long years where he had been mourning the lover he'd thought dead. Now she was here in his house, a few minutes earlier had been sitting on his bed in her nightgown, yet she seemed even further away from him than she ever had.

'It is for the best,' he told himself, although it was hard to believe as he lay there all alone in his huge bed. Surely Hetty's warm body by his side would be a better outcome.

With a sigh he rose. There was no way he'd be getting back to sleep any time soon. Illicit thoughts of Hetty were coursing through his mind, making him want to do something reckless.

Instead, he would immerse himself in work. A few hours studying the details of the horses he and Redfern had the chance to bid on would take his mind off things.

Chapter Eleven

Hetty had not slept well after her late-night wakening and the trip to Richard's room. Even when she was tucked up in bed again she'd kept imagining what could have happened if she had been a little bolder, a little less scared.

Her rational mind knew it had been the right thing to leave, to scurry back to her quiet, lonely bedroom, but her body had yearned for Richard.

'Mama, why are you still in bed?' Noah asked as he came barrelling through the door to her bedroom. He looked tousled and fresh from sleep and she felt a burst of love for him as he climbed into her bed and threw his arms around her neck. She inhaled, loving the sweet scent of him.

Although they had only been at Farnleigh Hall for a week, she could already see the change in him. Noah had always been a bright, energetic boy filled with love, but even at the tender age of two and a half he had learned to temper his enthusiasm and noise when Phillip was around. He had never received anything more than a gentle clip around the ear from the man he thought was his father, but that was enough for a small child to be cowed into submission. Hetty had fought Phillip on the two occasions he had laid a hand on her son, aware that from then on she had taken the blows that might otherwise have landed on Noah.

Here, in the safety of Farnleigh Hall, surrounded by people who were delighted with his presence, Noah was blossoming. He also had a healthy glow about him, no doubt from a week of good eating and exercise in the fresh air.

'Mama, I am going to see the horses.'

'Are you, my love?'

'Yes, I am going to feed them hay.'

'Well, be careful and make sure you feed them all the right amount.'

'Richard will help.' It was said in such a matter-of-fact way and Hetty realised the importance of reliability to a child of Noah's age. Every time Richard said he would do something with or for Noah he followed through. There were no empty promises. That meant more to Noah, even at his age, than any physical gift.

'I want breakfast,' Noah said, slipping from her arms and jumping off the bed.

'I need to dress, my love, and then I will join you for breakfast. You may play in the nursery until I am ready.'

Hetty dressed for the day, taking a moment to admire her still-new dress in the mirror before leaving her room. Noah was playing with his toy soldiers, but jumped up quickly at the sound of her approach, eager for his breakfast.

Farnleigh Hall had an extensive nursery that Hetty suspected had been designed for Richard and his three brothers, all close in age and needing space to play and learn as they grew. It was far too big for Noah alone, and as such they only used a few of the rooms. There was a small table in the main room of the nursery where Noah could have an early dinner, but breakfast was taken downstairs. Richard had insisted on it, telling her it was the most important meal of the day and the best time for everyone to sit down together. He'd informed her that his own parents had done the same with him and his brothers, leaving them to their nursemaids and tutors throughout the day but ensuring that everyone was together at breakfast.

When they arrived in the dining room Noah

slipped his hand from hers and ran to take a chair next to Richard.

'Good morning,' Richard said, smiling at his son fondly.

'Good morning!'

'What will it be this morning, Noah? Toast or eggs or both?'

'Both, both, both!' Noah chanted.

One of the maids stepped up to bring Noah some toast and Hetty took a seat next to her son to help him spread the butter.

'I trust you slept well?' Richard said.

Hetty looked up sharply before realising that Richard was speaking to Noah.

'I dreamed about my pony.'

'What was your pony like in your dream?'

'Big and strong like your horses. Brown with a star on his head.'

'He sounds like a magnificent pony. Do you still wish to feed the horses with me this morning?'

'Yes!' Noah bobbed up and down in excitement on his chair, stuffing a big piece of toast into his mouth in his excitement.

'Slow down, my darling,' Hetty said. She loved seeing him like this, happy and thriving.

'You could accompany us too,' Richard said quietly.

Hetty looked up in surprise. She had planned on quietly eating her breakfast then slipping away before she could be reminded of her conduct the night before. Richard was not the sort of man to bring up her behaviour in front of anyone else, but he must be thinking of how she had burst into his bedroom, laid her hands on his naked body and then almost kissed him. No wonder he'd felt the need to send her away.

'Yes, Mama will come too,' Noah said, beaming up at her then leaning sideways and resting his head against her chest.

'I do not want to impose.'

'It is no imposition. We will merely be feeding the horses.'

Hetty swallowed and then forced herself to meet Richard's gaze. He was sitting there at the head of the table looking completely unfazed, as if the night before had not happened.

She felt the first stirrings of embarrassment. He had told her that he had no interest in seducing her, no interest in picking up their relationship where they had left off. His reaction to her last night should be proof enough that he meant it.

Hetty took a bite of toast and chewed slowly. This should be a good thing. The last thing she wanted was the complication of romance in her life. She knew she would never be able to trust another man again, not after what Phillip had put her through. She should be rejoicing that Richard had actually listened to her and was not entertaining thoughts of rekindling their romance.

Yet his lack of interest in her made her feel unsettled, especially given her reaction to him in his bedroom the night before.

Silently, she told herself she could not have it both ways. Either she wanted his attention or she wanted his word that he would keep his distance. The two were not compatible.

With a sudden feeling of mortification, she realised that he might no longer be attracted to her at all. In addition to his promise to keep his distance, he might simply not desire her any longer. Hetty closed her eyes. The memory of Richard half naked with only a sheet covering his lower half came to her, interspersed with the images her mind had squirrelled away of him walking out of the lake, glistening and desirable. These last few years he had kept himself in prime physical shape, even after he'd left the army. In contrast, she had spent three years in poverty. No doubt he was used to mixing with young ladies who wore the latest fashion and had their hair dressed each and every day by their maids.

Self-consciously, Hetty placed a hand on her low bun. It was how she always wore her hair, pulled back from her face and fastened at the nape of her neck. It was practical and allowed her to go about her day without worrying that her hair would interfere with anything she needed to do, but she was aware that it was not as refined as the styles the women of Richard's class would wear.

Quietly she admonished herself. She was not of Richard's class and she could not change that. What was more, she should not be worrying what he thought of her appearance.

'Come, Noah, let us leave your mother to finish her breakfast in peace. Shall we meet you outside in ten minutes, Mrs Fairweather?'

'Yes, I will be ready then.'

Hetty watched them go, Noah's small hand in Richard's large one, hating the way her eyes were drawn to the way Richard's breeches fit snugly about the buttocks.

Behave, she told herself, sipping at the warm cup of tea and hoping that some fresh air might calm her. She did not want to do or say anything inappropriate, but her mind could not seem to move on from the attraction she felt bubbling under the surface.

'I want to race,' Noah announced, a big grin on his face. 'But I get to go first.'

'You want a head start?' Richard mused, looking down at his son with a smile.

'Yes. Me first. Then you two.'

Hetty held up her hands and laughed. 'I'm hardly dressed for racing.'

'You have to, Mama.'

'I'll give you a head start too,' Richard said. 'Although, from what I remember, you are very athletic.'

Hetty looked up sharply but there was only a look of innocence on his face. Today everything felt suggestive and she knew that was a problem with her, not the rest of the world.

'There should be a prize!' Noah said, already edging forwards.

'There should,' Richard agreed. 'How about ice cream for everyone, but the winner gets the biggest bowl?'

Noah jumped up and down in excitement.

'Are you ready, Noah?'

He nodded enthusiastically.

'Go!' Richard called, and they watched their son start to run, his little legs working hard as he crossed the grass between the house and the stables.

'I will let Noah have the victory, but I am coming for you, Mrs Fairweather,' Richard said, his lips close to her ear.

She turned and looked at him defiantly. 'Ten seconds head start and I can beat you.'

'You can have your ten seconds, but I will catch you.' His eyes twinkled in the sunlight and Hetty felt her pulse quicken.

His good humour was contagious. Ever since arriving at Farnleigh Hall she had felt the assault of kindness, but hadn't realised the effect on her. Even today, when she was tired and discombobulated, she felt herself smiling more in a few short minutes than she had in the previous three months. *That* was his gift. She supposed it was part of the reason he'd been such a good leader of men in the army. No matter how dire a situation, Richard had known how important it was to keep his men's spirits high. Melancholy soldiers could not hope of victory, but men who were bonded with their comrades, had shared a drink and a song with them, fought all the much harder for the man standing next to them.

'Ready?'

She nodded.

'Go!'

Hetty ran, focused on the target of the stable in front of her. Noah had just reached the building, slapping his hand on it in victory and letting out a little cheer of excitement. All too soon she heard Richard reach the count of ten behind her and then the thundering of his footsteps as he made chase.

At first she thought she might make it. Richard was fast, but she was light on her feet too. She made the mistake of looking over her shoulder when she was only a few feet from the stable wall. Turning round slowed her and Richard raced ahead, his hand slapping the brick of the outbuilding just seconds before hers.

'Mama runs fast,' Noah said, jumping up and down, 'but I'm faster.'

'You are,' Richard said, sweeping the little boy up into his arms and winking at Hetty. 'You will have the biggest bowl of ice cream this afternoon.'

'But first we feed the horses,' Noah said, suddenly looking serious.

'Yes, it is a big job, Noah. Are you up to it?'

The little boy wriggled out of Richard's arms and then stood to attention before him.

'Good. Let us get started.'

They entered the first of the outbuildings and Hetty was impressed by the size and cleanliness. She had been over to this part of the estate before, when she and Richard went for their ride a few days earlier, but she had not set foot inside the stables then, instead mounting her horse in the stable yard. This first building housed twelve horses, and as she peered out of the door at the other end she realised there were two more stables, slightly smaller but still a decent size.

'How many horses do you have, Lord Westbridge?'

'A fair number,' he said evasively.

'How many, exactly?'

He shrugged. 'Twenty-eight.'

'One more soon, with my pony,' Noah said as he skipped happily along between the rows of stalls.

'Twenty-eight horses!' Hetty's eyes widened in surprise. 'What could you want with twenty-eight horses?'

'Ask him how many grooms he employs to exercise the horses.' A voice came from behind them.

Hetty spun to see a smartly dressed man who looked vaguely familiar. He strode towards her with an air of confidence and stopped when he was a couple of feet away. He bowed deeply, as if he were greeting a member of the royal family.

'Mrs Fairweather, I doubt you remember me, but it is a pleasure to see you again.'

'Major Redfern,' Hetty said with a smile. 'Of course I remember you.' The Major had visited Richard when he was injured and had brought him news of what was happening in the ongoing skirmishes. Richard had always seemed buoyed by his presence and she was unsurprised they remained friends now.

'Excuse the intrusion. I see you are spending some time with young Noah.'

Hetty knew surprise must show on her face as Major Redfern saluted her son and Noah excitedly saluted back.

'Noah and I are about to help feed the horses. Is your business urgent?'

'No, nothing that cannot wait half an hour. You feed the horses. Mrs Fairweather, I wonder if you would care to accompany me on a stroll about the estate? We will not venture far in case Noah needs you.'

Hetty was a little taken aback at the suggestion, but after a quick glance at Noah to see he was already distracted by the horses she inclined her head.

They strolled out of the stables and along one of the paths that led from the formal gardens into the wider estate. It was another gloriously warm summer day and Hetty was glad of her bonnet, pulled down low to shield her eyes from the sun.

'How are you settling in at Farnleigh Hall?' Major Redfern enquired.

'Very well, thank you. Lord Westbridge has been most hospitable.'

'He is a good man.'

'What did you mean in the stables when you said to ask how many grooms he employed?'

'Ah, yes. A little joke, that is all.' At first it seemed that Major Redfern was not going to elaborate and then he looked at her and nodded. 'I suppose it is important you know what sort of man the Earl is.'

Hetty frowned, wondering what the implication behind his words was.

'Lord Westbridge loves horses. He is skilled at calming a frightened horse and is unrivalled on horseback. I have seen him leading many a charge into battle and he is unmatched in combat. When he left the army, it seemed likely he would continue to work with horses in some capacity.'

'That is what you are doing in your business venture together?'

'Yes and no. Together we are looking at breeding racehorses. My family have been involved in the buying and selling of horses for generations. I am using that expertise to find suitable animals for the stables.' He paused, turning back to motion at the stable. 'What Lord Westbridge is doing is much more noble. He has bought all these horses so that he may employ the grooms to look after them.'

'I do not understand.' Hetty frowned. Certainly horses needed grooms, that was not disputed.

'In the stables alone, Lord Westbridge employs twelve grooms and two stable boys. These men are all ex-soldiers, injured in some way in the war—

men who were struggling to support themselves in the world outside the army.'

Realisation began to dawn on Hetty. 'He keeps so many horses so he has enough work for the men.'

'Exactly. No man needs twenty-eight horses, not even Westbridge, but without them he would not be able to justify the jobs of so many. These men he employs, they want to work. They do not wish for charity; they wish to earn their money honestly.'

'I did not know,' Hetty said, wondering at the generosity of the act.

'There are more in the house, too. Did you not notice he has a vast number of servants for a single man living on his own? Farnleigh Hall is large, but it does not require six footmen and numerous maids.'

'He keeps such a large staff to provide employment?'

'Yes. Some injured soldiers, some are the widows or wives of men no longer able to work.'

'He is a good man. A selfless man.'

'He is,' Major Redfern said, fixing his gaze on Hetty.

She paused, then lifted her chin. She would not be intimidated by this man; she would not be intimidated by anyone ever again.

'If you have something you wish to say to me,

Major, I beg you to come straight out with it. There is no greater gift in this world than plain speaking.'

Major Redfern smiled at her request and nodded. 'I agree, Mrs Fairweather. It is perhaps best I just say what is on my mind.'

Hetty waited as the Major collected his thoughts. She knew the rough version of what he was going to say—how he was only trying to protect his friend, how he worried that she might hurt him.

'Lord Westbridge has been through more than most men are subjected to. First the terrible things he bore witness to whilst in the army, and then the deaths of his three brothers within such a short period of time.'

'He has had a tragic few years,' Hetty conceded.

'Added to this was the loss of you.' Major Redfern clasped his hands together behind his back as they continued walking slowly. He looked every inch the army officer, despite his civilian clothing. 'When he thought you dead, he was a husk of a man. His sense of duty and his loyalty and care for the men who served under him meant he got on with the business of fighting Napoleon, but underneath it all he was broken. He grieved for you deeply, despite the relatively short time you were acquainted.'

'I am sorry for that, but I do not think I can be held entirely at fault. I was injured and hit my head during the massacre and woke up to find I was the only person left alive in Cidade Velha do Douro.'

'No, you are right. It was an awful situation and none of it your fault. I also understand there was the complication of your husband.' Major Redfern sighed. 'I am not a pompous ass, Mrs Fairweather, despite how I might be coming across right now. I know people's lives are complicated and sometimes circumstance and coincidence scupper even the most devoted of relationships.'

'What is it you wish to say to me?'

'Please be careful with him. He is the best man I have ever had the pleasure of knowing. He is strong, but he has suffered so much. I do not think he could bear to lose any more.'

'Lord Westbridge and I…' Hetty began, but Major Redfern held up his hands.

'I do not need to know the details. I think it best I do not. Your relationship was always complex, even in Portugal. I see how he looks at the son you share, and I know how he felt about you.'

'I am not planning on taking Noah away from him.' Hetty let out a little disbelieving laugh. 'I wouldn't be so cruel.'

'What if things turn sour between you?'

'They will not,' Hetty said quickly. 'And if they

did, I am not so heartless I would keep Lord Westbridge from Noah.'

'Yet you did not inform him about his son, or that you lived for three years.'

Hetty struggled to contain the anger that welled up inside her. 'I will forgive you for your bluntness as I know you are only concerned for Lord Westbridge's welfare, but you overstep, Major Redfern. You know nothing of me, of what I have lived through these last few years, what my life has been. Yet you assume so many things about my character because of the decisions I have been forced to make.'

He studied her face and then seemed to concede. 'You are right, of course. I have been unbelievably rude. I worry about Westbridge and I know what happened the last time he loved and lost you. I do not wish him to go through it again, but that does not excuse my words.'

Hetty nodded, wanting nothing more than to get away. She knew her actions in the past had hurt Richard, but heartbreak had been an inevitable outcome as soon as Phillip had reappeared, rising from the dead like an unwanted spirit.

'I think you have said everything you could possibly need to, Major Redfern, and now I will take my leave. Please tell Lord Westbridge I have returned to the house and that I will be waiting for Noah once he has finished feeding the horses.'

Before the Major had a chance to reply she spun and strode off, heading towards Farnleigh Hall. Her heart was pounding in her chest and there were tears in her eyes, but she made sure to keep a straight back and an even pace so Major Redfern would not see how shaken she actually was.

Chapter Twelve

'Where is she?' Richard stormed through the house, flinging open doors searching for Hetty. Noah had been safely left in the garden playing with his new nursemaid, and now all Richard could think about was Hetty.

Redfern had returned sheepishly to the stables, admitting he had perhaps gone too far when warning Hetty not to abandon Richard again. He could imagine the scenario, his friend enthusiastically regaling Hetty with tales of how heartbroken Richard had been when he had thought her dead. How nothing had seemed to matter, how he had withdrawn into himself. Only his sense of duty, his responsibility for the men who'd served under him had pulled him through. Redfern would have thought he was doing Richard a service, ensuring Hetty wasn't going to trample all over his heart again, but he did not know all the details. He did not know that Hetty had spent the last three years being manipulated and abused by the person who should have cherished and protected her.

From the apologetic way he had explained things to Richard, no doubt Hetty had felt Redfern's words an attack.

Richard had finished feeding the horses with Noah, aware that Hetty would not want him to cut their time together short when Noah had been so looking forward to it, then he had brought Noah back to his nursemaid so he could check on Hetty alone.

He rushed up the stairs to the third floor, trying to remember which room of the many up on this level Hetty had chosen for her own. It had been the bedroom closest to the nursery and without thinking he threw open the door and burst inside.

Hetty screamed and Richard froze, unable to move.

She was reclining in the bath, hair loose about her shoulders, looking the most ravishing he had ever seen her.

'Hetty... I...' he stammered, knowing he should turn around. Finally, his body obeyed the commands coming from his brain and he turned, clutching at the doorframe to try to steady himself. 'Forgive me,' he said.

She still hadn't spoken, hadn't made a sound since

her initial scream, but he knew he had to leave and explain things when she was dressed.

Swallowing hard, he stepped from the room, reaching behind him for the door handle so he did not have to turn around.

His heart pounded in his chest. There had been something about her scream that threatened to drag him back to the darkness that was always bubbling under the surface. The war had changed him in innumerable ways, but the worst thing that lingered was this sense of doom, this overwhelming despair and fear that sometimes coursed through him. It could be triggered by anything—often something innocuous. His body would be flooded with panic and fear and sometimes even images of the worst things he had seen, the things that haunted him still, flashed through his mind.

It was not something that he could control, although thankfully as time passed the episodes became less frequent, but he doubted he would ever be rid of it.

Now he stood in the corridor, head pressed against the wall, breathing deeply and willing the moment to pass.

Downstairs in his study, Richard poured a generous measure of brandy and threw it back, despite it not being much past eleven o'clock in the morning. His senses were beginning to return to normal and after ten minutes he had himself under control.

Hetty took her time and it was almost noon before she appeared in his study. He stood, his eyes raking over her, unable to stop himself from remembering what he had seen when she was in the bath.

'You're imagining me naked,' she said, her voice calm and quiet, her expression neutral.

Richard cleared his throat, getting ready to deny it, but he found he could not lie to her. 'I am.'

For a long thirty seconds they both stared at one another, a pulse of desire and angst throbbing between them. Richard stepped closer, narrowing the gap, but stopped before he was close enough to touch her.

'Forgive me. I have not lived with a woman in…' He broke off and laughed. 'Well…ever. At least not since childhood.'

'You did not think I might be enjoying the privacy of my room?'

'I never thought you might be bathing. Are you mad at me?' He searched her face for an answer and was surprised to see more amusement than anger. Hetty was a complex woman to understand. She flew into a rage about him burning her flea-infested dress, flinched at his innocent touch, but did not seem to mind that he had burst into her bedroom uninvited and seen her naked in the bath.

'There is no harm done,' she said eventually. 'And it is not as if it is anything you have not seen before.' She shrugged. 'Although my body has changed since you were familiar with it.'

Inhaling sharply, Richard could not stop his gaze from dipping down momentarily to take in the curve of her waist and the swell of her breasts.

'What was so urgent that you needed to burst into my room in such a fashion?'

'Redfern told me of your conversation. I thought he would have upset you. He had no right to say the things he did.'

'I admit I was upset. As soon as I was out of his sight, I ran all the way back to the house. Sarah, my lady's maid—' she scoffed at the idea of her having a lady's maid then continued '—came upon me as I entered through the front door and suggested a bath to calm me.'

'Did it work?'

'Until some rogue came bursting into my *private* bedchamber and saw me laid out in my nakedness, the only thing to protect my dignity the water.'

'Again, apologies.'

'Redfern was harsh, but I think his words were

motivated by love. Not that his motivation excuses his rudeness.'

'He questioned your reason for being here?'

'No.' Hetty cocked her head to one side. 'That he did not do. Although perhaps he would have asked me if your vast fortune had influenced my coming here if I had not left so abruptly.' She sagged a little. 'He is worried you will grow attached to me or Noah, or both, and then I will leave.'

Richard swallowed. That was his fear, although he had never voiced it to his friend. Redfern was a perceptive man and had been there to pick up the pieces when Richard had been hit with bereavement after bereavement over the last few years.

Looking up at him with her keen brown eyes, Hetty considered him for a moment. 'I cannot promise to never leave, Richard.'

'I know.'

'But I do promise never to stop you from having a relationship with your son.'

'Thank you. Your vow means a lot to me.' Of course, anything could happen to Noah, but when he was with his son he forced himself not to always think the worst. Just because his brothers had all died didn't mean he was cursed to lose others that he cared for.

Richard's eyes swept over the woman in front of

him and he felt the urge to wrap her in his arms. He wanted to protect her too, to hide her away from the world so nothing bad could happen to her, but he knew she was not his to protect. Even if she had been, he knew better than to believe he could prevent all harm from reaching her. No, he was better to focus his attention on Noah, provide Hetty with whatever material things she needed from him but keep his heart closed off. Even if it clamoured to be heard, for him to acknowledge he still had deep-seated feelings for Hetty.

He reached out without thinking and took her hand in his, only realising she hadn't flinched at his touch after their fingers were intertwined. Hetty must have noticed too for a look of bewilderment crossed her face.

In that moment he had the urge to kiss her, despite his resolve only seconds earlier to commit to a platonic relationship. She looked so bemused, so lost, that he wanted to gather her in his arms and kiss her until she could think of nothing but him and his touch. It was the same feeling he'd experienced the night before, when she had sat on the edge of his bed, that crashing desire that obscured all reason and made him think only of pleasure and not the consequences.

His desire was not helped by the fact that Hetty

took an unwitting step towards him, her eyes fixed on his, her lips parted slightly. If he didn't know better, he would have believed she was feeling the same as him. He had an inescapable urge to kiss her and never stop.

His eyes searched hers for an answer, but before he could reach any conclusion she turned away.

'I should check on Noah,' she murmured and then walked so quickly from the room that Richard thought it looked as if she was fleeing.

Chapter Thirteen

The day was warm and bright and Richard's mood was jubilant as the carriage trundled along the country roads. He would prefer to be on horseback, but it was not practical with Hetty and Noah accompanying him for their trip.

The journey to the ruined and abandoned Dunstanburgh Castle would take them three hours in good conditions, and where they had not had any rain for weeks the roads were hardened and allowed for the carriage to move quickly. As it would take so long, they had agreed to take a picnic to enjoy on the beach and Richard had booked rooms at a local inn so they could rest the night there and make the return journey the next day.

He was in good spirits, reminded of his trips to the seaside with his older brothers when he was young. Once his brothers had reached school age and he was left behind at home he had impatiently waited for the holidays, knowing as soon as his brothers returned they would scoop him up and together ride out to one of the beaches, sometimes even sleeping under the stars for a night. They were some of his fondest memories.

He doubted Noah would remember this. Most of his early memories were when he was five or six, but he was a firm believer in laying down a solid foundation. He hated to think of what damage might have been done already to Noah's developing brain by witnessing the violence from the man he thought his father towards his mother, and from living in fear in that house. He comforted himself by thinking of the love Noah had received from Hetty, and the knowledge that she would have done anything to shield him from the worst of her late husband's behaviour.

'Mama, I can see the sea!' Noah said, his voice high with excitement.

Richard watched as Hetty leaned over her son to look out of the window.

'Look! A castle!' The little boy's voice was almost a shriek now and Richard smiled as he saw the crumbling form of Dunstanburgh Castle come into view.

Twenty minutes later, the carriage rolled to a stop around half a mile away from the castle.

'We need to walk over the dunes to reach the castle itself,' Richard explained as they climbed down from the carriage.

'Shall I set up a picnic on the beach, my lord?' Whitely had accompanied them on the trip to carry the hamper of food and ensure everything went smoothly. He had sat up top with the coachman and, for most of the trip, Miss Leven, Noah's nursemaid. Miss Leven had started the journey inside the carriage, but had felt nauseous from the swaying motion and had soon retreated to the fresh air.

Richard felt a swell of love as Noah gripped hold of his hand, holding his mother's hand on the other side.

'Lead the way, my lord,' Hetty said. She had relaxed in his company these last few days, and she seemed happier. He hoped it was because she felt safe. He wanted to provide that for her—a haven where she could lick her wounds and heal.

Now, all he needed to do was quiet the flare of desire he felt whenever she was near. It had been overwhelming ever since she had woken him from his nightmare, his fantasy of her in his bed returning whenever she stood close. It was a purely physical reaction, he was sure of it, and he knew these things could be conquered. Richard had never failed at something he set his mind to. If he deemed it vitally important, he would try and try again until he came upon the right solution. It would be the same here. *Something* would help banish the thoughts that plagued him.

If he could suppress the desire he felt for her, they could fall into a comfortable routine where they both spent time with Noah, together and apart. He was kept busy with estate business, searching for horses to add to his stables and his work of trying to help those the army or the navy had abandoned after discharge. Soon he hoped to broach the idea with Hetty that she might like to help him with the latter. If she agreed, it would be something else to keep her busy, to tie her to the area.

Richard grimaced, aware that he was trying to organise everything to be exactly how he wanted it, but other people rarely had identical views to his. He needed to tread carefully, ensure he did not scare her off. That was another reason why he needed to take control of the attraction he felt for Hetty. The last thing he wanted was for her to feel driven away because he could not control his baser urges.

The walk through the dunes to the castle was glorious. It was a hot day but the wind from the sea whipped at them and cooled the air, meaning they were refreshed when they reached the entrance to the castle.

Noah was thrilled as they approached the heavy

wooden door and Richard pushed it open. 'Do knights live inside?' he asked, his eyes flitting between the towers that flanked the entrance.

'They did once, a long time ago. No one has lived here for many years now. That is why we are allowed inside.'

They stepped through the archway together and Richard felt his heart sing as Noah looked around in awe.

'Can we climb the towers?'

'Only if you are very careful and hold my hand all the way up.'

'I promise,' Noah said, gripping his hand even tighter.

They spent the next hour exploring, Richard careful to take into consideration Noah's young age, often lifting him over the bigger obstacles. Miss Leven had taken the opportunity to sit on a section of the castle wall whilst her services were not needed, but Hetty accompanied him and Noah, sometimes climbing with them and sometimes motioning for them to go ahead without her.

The last part of the castle he wanted to show Noah was a tower that overlooked the sea. There was a huge step up to get onto the spiral staircase, but once they were on it, Noah's legs could manage the stairs.

'I don't think I can make it up there,' Hetty said, calling up after them.

'Let me show Noah the view, and then I will help you up once he is safely back with Miss Leven. I think this the finest vista in England.'

He spent some time with Noah, pointing out the features of the coastline to the north and south before they climbed back down. Hetty was waiting a little distance away for them.

'I will take Noah to Miss Leven, then you must come see the view.'

'It's high, Mama,' Noah said, skipping alongside his father as they returned to the nursemaid.

'Sit here with Miss Leven whilst I take your mother up the tower to see the view.'

Noah nodded, sitting close to the young woman and starting to tell her about all the things he had seen.

Satisfied he was cared for, Richard made his way back to the edge of the cliff and the tower that was perched upon it.

'Are you ready to see the magnificence of Northumberland?' He held out a hand to Hetty and felt a surge of happiness as she took it without hesitation. A few weeks ago, it had seemed as if they would never be able to touch, not even innocently like this. 'The first step up is the biggest, then it is just a normal staircase.' He hopped up first and then turned to help Hetty up.

As they ascended the stairs he felt the wind whip around his ears and smiled. He had not thought it possible that one day he might visit one of these sights he had once enjoyed with his brothers and feel anything but sadness, but today here with Noah and Hetty he felt joy.

'That is quite a view,' Hetty said as they stood at the top of the tower. The wind had pulled loose some of her hair and now it danced around her face as she looked out over the gentle waves of the sea. To the south was the rolling coastline, to the north the sand of Dunstanburgh beach and the cliffs beyond.

Without thinking, Richard reached out and tucked the stray loose hairs behind her ear, saving her cheeks from the onslaught. It was an intimate gesture, too intimate, and he started voicing an apology as Hetty turned to him.

Something in her eyes stopped him and for a long moment they stood face to face at the top of the tower, contemplating one another.

The moment was broken by a shout from Miss Leven and they both looked down immediately. To Richard's horror, he saw Noah running towards the cliff edge. Somehow, he had got away from Miss Leven and from where she was at the castle entrance there was no way she would catch him. He seemed to be chasing something, a fluttering shape that Richard could not make out from this distance.

He reacted immediately, throwing himself down the spiral staircase, taking the steps three at a time. If Noah chased whatever it was over the cliff it would be the end of him. The drop was sheer, twenty feet to the rocks below, and if the little boy was focused on something else he might not notice the approaching cliff edge.

Richard ran faster than he had ever run before, his feet kicking up the grass behind him, his heart pounding, until, a few feet away from the cliff edge, he lunged forward and swept Noah up into his arms.

Noah looked up, perplexed.

'You were a little close to the edge there,' Richard said, showing the boy the drop. He didn't want to scare him, but felt it would irresponsible not to at least try to teach Noah a little basic safety.

Hetty ran up to them and grabbed Noah from his arms, holding their son tight to her chest. He could see the colour had drained from her face and her hands were shaking as she caressed Noah's back.

'Don't squeeze,' Noah said, squirming.

Gently she set him back on the ground, but gripped his hand firmly.

'I'm so sorry, my lord. He just ran.'

Richard did his best to suppress the anger he felt towards the nursemaid. She was wringing her hands and looked sick with worry.

'There was no harm done this time,' he said, his voice hard, 'but please do not take your eyes off him in future. He is only two and a half.'

'Yes, my lord.'

Hetty's heart had still not stopped thumping in her chest. When she had seen Noah running towards the cliff edge she had feared the worst. All this time, she had kept him safe from the threat of her late husband, and now, on a much anticipated trip, she had almost lost him. Never had she seen a person move so fast as Richard. It was as if he had been driven by a supernatural force, watched over by an angel. When he had scooped Noah up into his arms she'd felt a crashing sense of relief.

Now, she wasn't sure she would ever be able to let Noah out of her sight again.

'Please walk ahead to the beach and ensure everything is ready for lunch,' she said to Miss Leven.

She did not want to be around the nursemaid until her anger had abated as she might say something she regretted. Miss Leven's one job was to protect Noah and to fail so miserably on one of their first trips out was almost unforgivable. Hetty was unconvinced that Miss Leven was the right person to be in charge of Noah's care, but she knew she had to give the young woman a chance. Sometimes she seemed a little abrupt with Noah, and Hetty wondered if she had experience in looking after a child as young as Noah—she did not seem to know what level of supervision was required. Another week or two should be enough to see if the nursemaid would settle into the role or if they would need to look for someone else.

Noah was quiet on the walk down to the beach, but he held her hand the whole way without moaning. Even if he didn't understand the seriousness of the situation he was certainly picking up on her mood.

She felt a little less nervous when they reached the beach and were far away from any cliffs with perilous drops, but everything felt dangerous now. Noah could run in the waves and be swept out to sea, or become excited to see the horses with the carriage and dart out and get trampled underfoot.

When they reached the little picnic area that Whitely had set out Hetty sat down on the blanket and held Noah against her chest, relaxing a little as she felt his heart beating steadily away. They ate, Noah delighting in the cakes Cook had packed for him, and then he collapsed exhausted onto the blanket and fell fast asleep.

Miss Leven sat awkwardly off to one side and Hetty was thankful when Richard suggested the nursemaid take a walk amongst the dunes.

Now it was just her and Richard and a sleeping Noah, and when they were certain he was fast asleep Hetty stood and motioned for Richard to join her a few feet away.

'Thank you,' she said, standing close so she could speak quietly in a bid not to disturb Noah. The wind picked up her words and carried them away, but from Richard's expression she saw he had heard them.

'You never need to thank me for keeping our boy safe.'

'Without you…' Hetty let the words hang in the air.

'Do not think about it. Nothing bad happened. Noah is here with us, completely safe.'

'But what if…'

'Hetty,' he said, taking both her hands in his own. She was surprised to find his touch comforting, reassuring. For so long, any physical contact had made her fear for what came next, but in a few short weeks Richard had cured her of that fear. His relentless kindness, his respect for her boundaries, it all meant that she was no longer waiting to be hurt all the time.

'Our boy is safe. Do not torture yourself thinking of any other scenario.'

Before she could stop herself, Hetty reached up and placed a hand on Richard's cheek. Her pulse quickened and she felt a deep desire for this man. There was no denying he was physically attractive, but she knew right now what she found so desirable was his willingness to do whatever it took to protect her and her son. It was seductive.

Rising up on her tiptoes, she brushed a kiss against his lips. It was gentle and hesitant, but filled with three years of longing. At first Richard did not react, stunned by the unexpected intimacy, and then he groaned and pulled her closer to him. He kissed her properly then, long and hard and deep, one hand tangled in her hair, the other on her back, holding her close.

They kissed as if they had never been apart and Hetty felt the desire she had been suppressing these last few weeks crash over her. If Richard had suggested they lay on the beach and made love she would not have been able to resist.

For a moment she wondered if everything could be this simple. If she gave in to the desire that coursed through her and surrendered to the happiness she knew Richard could give her. She was no longer jumping at every physical contact; perhaps he could help heal her other mental scars as well.

Even as she had the thought she knew it was too much of a burden to place on one man. Richard had been through enough; he did not need to be saddled with an emotionally crippled woman who might not be able to give him the affection and love he deserved. He was not her doctor, and she could not ask him to take a chance on her.

Slowly, she pulled away.

'I'm sorry,' she said, her eyes searching his face for some sign, something that would allow her to dive back into his arms.

'That was unexpected,' Richard murmured. He caressed her cheek, trailed his fingers down onto her neck, and Hetty closed her eyes. She could not bear to disappoint him and she wished things could be different.

'It shouldn't have happened,' she said, taking a step back.

Richard looked at her warily.

'Forgive me,' Hetty said, half turning away. 'I was overcome with emotion, but I shouldn't have done that.'

He straightened, stepping back. 'No harm has been done,' he said stiffly, the pain visible in his eyes.

'Richard, I…'

He didn't give her a chance to explain, to tell him that she wanted him but she was pulling away for his own protection. She wasn't sure she would ever be able to love again, and Richard deserved a woman who could love him with every inch of her.

'No,' he said, a tight smile on his lips. 'We shall speak of it no more. You check on Noah. I will ensure the coach is ready to take us to our inn.'

Chapter Fourteen

Aware that he was liable to wear the floorboards out with his pacing, Richard still could not stop. His room at the inn was comfortable but not large and he only managed four and a half strides from one wall to the other before he had to turn back and go the other way. Sitting still was not an option. He needed to be moving, to distract his tortured brain at least a little.

He was a fool. A confused fool. On the beach he'd wanted to kiss Hetty. He'd been wanting to kiss her for weeks. If he was completely honest with himself, he'd wanted to kiss her ever since she'd walked back into his study and he'd been confronted with the fact that she was not dead.

The episode on the beach had been more romantic than that, though. They had both been tense, emotions high since Noah's near accident, and he'd felt the bond between them as they'd stood face to face.

Then she'd kissed him. There was no doubt about it, no uncertainty as to who had initiated the kiss. He'd been standing completely still and she had risen up onto her tiptoes and kissed him. And it had felt so right.

'It was so wrong,' he muttered, clenching and unclenching his fists by his sides.

He could understand her reaction if *he* had kissed *her*, but that wasn't what had happened at all. She'd looked at him misty-eyed, she'd caressed his cheek, she'd reached up and kissed him. Admittedly, he'd been the one to take it further, to pull her in close and turn the gentle meeting of their lips into something much more, but given what he felt for the woman it was hardly surprising.

He had been ready to ravish her on the beach. During their short affair whilst in Portugal they'd had to be inventive in finding time alone together and it wouldn't have been the first time he'd lain with her outdoors. Yet, instead of ripping each other's clothes off, she'd said *Oops*.

Well, not exactly, but the sentiment was the same.

Now he was frustrated and confused. Why had she kissed him if she did not want any intimacy between them? She'd spent the last few weeks making it painfully clear they would not be resuming the relationship they had enjoyed in Portugal. He'd respected that decision, working to find ways they could enjoy one another's company and give Noah exactly what he needed whilst eschewing the intimate, loving part of their relationship. Then she'd gone and kissed him.

Richard forced himself to stop pacing, leaning instead against the mantelpiece with one arm, his head resting in the crook of his elbow.

This was why he had to keep his distance from her. Both emotionally and physically. He could not be at her whim. His heart would not stand it. Already he had lost too much and if he were to open his heart to Hetty, only to have her leave or decide she did not want a close relationship, it would break him once and for all.

It was the right decision, but he knew if she came hurrying along the corridor telling him she had made a terrible mistake he would struggle to keep his resolve.

Just as he had the thought there was a gentle rap on the door.

'Who is it?'

'Mrs Fairweather.' Hetty's voice was hesitant, as if she knew she should not be there.

Richard flung open the door and looked her up and down. She looked beautiful, still windswept from their time at the coast, her cheeks flushed.

'No,' he said before she could say any more. 'We share a child. We shared a bed. When it is just the two of us, I will not be calling you Mrs Fairweather.'

Hetty bristled. 'It is my name and the rules of Society…'

'Damn the rules of Society. Come in.' He ushered her into the room, checking the corridor to ensure no one was watching who might gossip.

'Noah is asleep.'

'Good.'

She cleared her throat. 'I owe you an explanation. And an apology.'

'I don't want your apology.'

He closed the door behind her and turned, suddenly acutely aware that they were alone in a very small space, with the only real piece of furniture a double bed.

'I want to give it anyway.'

He sighed and then motioned for her to sit down. Hetty perched on the edge of the bed and he took a spot close to the window, leaning against the wide windowsill.

'I realise I have not been the most consistent in my speech and my behaviour,' Hetty began. 'I was rather abrupt in how I told you I had no desire to rekindle our romantic relationship.'

Richard ran a hand across his brow. He was a patient man, an understanding man for the most part, but he did not want to hear the details of this.

'Perhaps you could skip ahead,' he said. 'I have rather a bad headache and I don't think any of this is going to make it better.'

'I was not lying when I said I could not imagine being touched again. When I first arrived here I felt battered and bruised, even though all my physical wounds have long since healed. Every loud noise made me jump and every touch made me flinch.' She smiled softly at him and he had to remind himself that he was angry with her. 'What I didn't count on was your kindness, how you gave me my space, slowly opened me up to the idea of trust again. It was liberating to feel you touch me in innocuous ways, our hands accidentally brushing together as we walked. It felt as though I was regaining my liberty, my joy again.'

Richard looked up, pushing aside his feelings of anger and irritation. For the first time Hetty was properly opening up to him, telling him how she felt, and despite recent events he did want to hear this.

Hetty laughed, but there was more sadness in the sound than humour. 'All these years I thought my happiness a thing of the past, and then I spend a few weeks with you and you break through the barriers

I have erected and make me feel things I never believed I would ever feel again.'

'I am happy to have helped in some small way,' he said, no note of bitterness in his voice now. 'I do not wish for you to be sad, Hetty.'

'I also think it is necessary I confess that I felt something akin to desire for you,' Hetty said and Richard's head snapped up. It was gratifying to hear. In a situation such as this, it was easy to start believing that one had misread the other person's feelings.

'"Something akin to desire"?'

Colour rushed to her cheeks and Hetty cleared her throat. 'Desire,' she said softly, holding his eye this time. 'The same desire that I could not deny in Portugal. It builds between us whenever you are close. Normally I have control of it, but today, with the heightened emotions after the danger Noah was in…' She spread her hands. 'It got away from me.'

'That is why we kissed?'

'Yes.'

He nodded, unsure what to make of this. There was no talk of love, no mention of the deep care and respect they had for one another alongside the desire. Silently, Richard realised he had made the right decision. In another life, he and Hetty would have been very happy, but the circumstances were not right now. She could not love him, not after everything she had been through. He thought perhaps he did still love her, but a one-sided love was not something to fight for. It would breed resentment and discord and eventually it would break them. Better they suppress the desire and he forget his deeper feelings. They might never find happiness together, but it would leave them free to pursue it apart.

'You wish to make sure it never happens again?'

'Yes.' Her eyes flicked to his lips as she spoke and he knew instinctively that she was thinking about kissing him right now. 'I'm sorry, Richard.' He smiled wryly at the use of his Christian name.

'We have made one another no promises. There is nothing to be sorry for.'

'I should not have kissed you.'

'But you did, and it cannot be undone. I will strive to forget it ever happened.'

That would be impossible.

He wondered for a moment if they could find a way to enjoy one another physically without emotional complications. It would satisfy his need for her, the deep longing that he felt every time she was near. Perhaps it would slake her desire for him too.

He cleared his throat, searching for the right words. Normally, he was quick-witted and articulate but in this moment words failed him. He felt as if he were lumbering through a forest blindfolded, unable to see the best direction to take.

'Thank you,' Hetty said quietly, but did not get up to move. He wondered if she'd had the same thought, the way to satisfy their lust without tying them together for ever.

'We are both consenting adults,' Richard said slowly, looking up to gauge her reaction, 'neither of us currently committed to another. And we have been intimate before.'

For a moment Hetty's expression did not change and then her eyes widened.

'If we did share a night of intimacy it is not as if we would be committing a sin we have not perpetrated before.'

She did not immediately flee from the room at his suggestion, so Richard pressed on.

'I agree with you that a romantic entanglement with each other is not what we need, but we both admit the desire we feel for one another can be… distracting.'

'You're proposing we spend the night together, and then continue as if nothing had happened?'

Richard shrugged. 'Perhaps it is what we need. To exorcise the desire we feel. One night, no expectations of anything more than that.'

'You would be satisfied with that?'

'It is not a ploy to drive you into my arms for eternity. As hard as I find it to admit, I agree we are not best suited in our current states, not as we were three years ago. Yet I find myself unable to think of anything but you whenever you are close.'

'And I you,' Hetty murmured.

Richard stood and moved closer to the bed. Hetty stood to meet him. They were face to face, only an inch separating their bodies. She bit her lip and he couldn't quite believe she was seriously considering his proposal. Yet he could see she felt the same desire he did, yearned for his touch as he did hers.

Gently he raised a hand and traced it up the length of her back.

'Tomorrow we would return to normal? Pretend this never happened?'

Nodding, he closed the gap between them, loving the way she fitted perfectly against his body. Somewhere deep inside, Richard knew this was a bad idea, but all he could think of was spending the night with the woman he had dreamed about for so long. He was a man of strong character. Surely, if he told himself that once was all they could have, his resolve and self-control would allow him to stick with it.

'It's a bad idea, Richard,' Hetty said, her face buried in his neck, but despite her words she did not pull away.

'Tell me you don't want this.'

'I can't.'

'Tell me you want to stop.'

'I can't.'

Eventually, she looked up at him, her expression filled with desire, and he knew, however unwise, neither of them would be able to be the one who pulled away.

Hetty wondered when she had become so reckless. Standing here, her body pressed against Richard's, she could think of nothing else but how it would feel to spend at least some of the night in his arms. She wanted to be kissed by him, touched by him, to make love until all rational thoughts were driven away.

Tomorrow be damned, she would deal with that when it came. Tonight she wanted to feel the exquisite pleasure of Richard's touch.

Knowing she would have to make the first move, Hetty pulled away slightly and then rose up on tiptoe, hesitating when her lips were a hair's breadth from his. Richard was too chivalrous to kiss her first, but she knew once she had touched her lips to his he would take control.

Relishing the moment, she swayed forward and

kissed him. It was as if something had been ignited inside him as their lips met. His arms tightened around her waist, his hands trailing over her body, claiming her.

He spun her round and pulled at the fastenings that held her dress together, making much shorter work of them than her maid. Within seconds her dress was pooled on the ground and she was left standing in her chemise and petticoats.

'I have imagined this moment more times than you could ever believe,' he murmured as he kissed her neck, sending waves of pleasure through her body. Hetty felt as though she were on fire, her skin burning at his touch, and with every kiss wanting more.

She ran her hands over his arms, his back, pulling his shirt from the waistband of his trousers. His body felt familiar, and with a rush of desire Hetty remembered what it was like to have him pressed against her as he entered her. As he pulled the shirt over his head and discarded it somewhere on the floor behind him, Hetty placed her hands on his chest. She wanted to become reacquainted with every single part of him.

He groaned as her fingers moved down towards his waistband and she could see his hardness pressing against the material of his trousers. It gave her a thrill of pleasure to think that she was the one responsible for his arousal, that despite everything that had happened in the last three years he still found her attractive.

'My turn,' he said, kissing her again and then releasing her from her petticoats. Only her chemise remained; made of the thinnest cotton, it barely hid what was beneath. Richard paused, resting his hands on her waist before he scrunched the material of her chemise in his hands and whipped it off over her head.

She stood naked before him, her body throbbing with anticipation as he raked his eyes over her.

'You grow more beautiful,' he murmured and then stepped forward and kissed her again, this time long and deep until Hetty felt her head spin.

Carefully, he lifted her onto the bed, settling her back on the pillows as he positioned himself above her. Her hand moved to his waistband but he swatted her away, taking both of her wrists and holding them above her head.

'All in good time,' he said with a smile and then lowered his lips to meet her skin. Within seconds Hetty was moaning and within a minute her body was writhing beneath his touch. He moved slowly, kissing and nipping until she was worked into a frenzy, begging him to give her some release. 'What is it you want?'

Hetty's tongue flicked out to wet her lips. It was a torturous question and he knew it. She wanted *everything*. She wanted him to possess her until all she could think about was pleasure and all she could scream was his name.

'Perhaps for me to touch you here?'

She inhaled sharply as his fingers dipped between her legs, grazing against her.

'You always did like that,' he said, his fingers moving slowly, rhythmically. Hetty felt her hips coming up to meet him as she begged him to go faster. 'We have time, my love.'

She barely noticed the term of endearment, but her brain stored it away to mull over later.

Hetty was lost. A wonderful pressure was building inside her and with every stroke, every touch, she grew closer to losing control. With a low moan she felt the waves of pleasure pulse through her, obliterating all rational thought and carrying her away.

It took her thirty seconds to return fully to her body and as she did she grabbed at Richard's hips, pulling him towards her. Finally, she slipped her hand under his waistband, enjoying his groan of anticipation as her fingers closed around his manhood.

Now she was fully in control and she loved how

she could make him moan in pleasure just by moving her fingers backwards and forwards.

She guided him between her legs and as he pushed inside her she felt as if she were whole again for the first time in three years.

Richard had always been a good lover, attentive to her needs, aware how much she enjoyed being teased and brought to the very edge and now it was as if they had never been apart. Over and over their bodies came together until Hetty felt the tension build inside her again and then as Richard thrust into her one last time she succumbed to her own climax.

Something Hetty had always loved about being intimate with Richard was the way he held her afterwards, and today was no different, despite this being a very different situation to when they had been together three years earlier. He manoeuvred himself so he was lying next to her and pulled her in close.

As they lay body to body Hetty felt a contentment she hadn't felt for a long time. Soon she would have to rouse herself and creep back to her room where Noah and Miss Leven were sleeping, hoping that the nursemaid would not have noticed her absence, but for now she was going to enjoy the feelings of security and happiness that were coursing through her body.

Chapter Fifteen

Richard had been unable to sleep once Hetty had left his bedroom. The bed had seemed cold and empty without her and already he was yearning for her touch.

It had been supremely foolish to think that one night with her, not even a full night, would be enough to slake the lust he had been feeling. If anything, it had just inflamed it.

Pulling on his jacket, he stepped out into the corridor and made his way silently out of the inn. It was only a little after six in the morning so, apart from one serving girl who was already working hard in the kitchen, there was no one else about, which suited Richard just fine. He needed fresh air and solitude and a good long walk on the beach.

He made his way down to the dunes, walking briskly. It was cool this morning, in the way it was when there had been a clear sky at night, allowing the temperature to plummet. He relished the chill in the air and the wind that whipped at his collar. Growing up in Northumberland, he was well accustomed to both and it was a welcome reminder that he was home.

Richard felt torn. He had been the one to suggest their one night of passion, and if he was completely honest with himself it had been a completely selfish act that allowed him to act on the desire he felt with no consequences. Or at least that had been the plan. Of course there would be consequences. Their relationship would shift and change because of it.

'I hope it was worth it,' he murmured to himself, and then felt a jolt of irritation. It had been worth it. Deep inside, he knew he was not satisfied with the awkward relationship between him and Hetty. He could pretend, but last night had only served to highlight how he wanted more. He wanted what they had shared in Portugal. A relationship between equals, between two people free to give all of themselves to one another.

Hetty protested that she would not be able to love again after what her late husband had put her through, but so much had changed already in the few short weeks she had been at Farnleigh Hall with him. When she had arrived, she was skittish and jumping at every loud noise, every physical touch. Now she sought his touch, revelled in it.

Surely all she needed was time.

Richard reached the top of the dunes and paused, taking deep breaths of the salty sea air.

He would not rush things, not press her for a decision, but he was not going to pretend any longer that he did not want her to share every aspect of his life.

In the distance he caught sight of two figures walking along the beach and immediately he knew it was Hetty and Noah. He frowned, wondering why they were out so early, but reasoned that Noah was an early riser and there wasn't much to entertain a young child in a single room in an inn.

They hadn't seen him as he approached and he took a moment to marvel at the scene in front of him. *This* was what he wanted: Hetty carefree and happy and his son revelling in love from both of them.

As soon as he'd had the thought it was followed quickly by another. *They'll be taken from you.*

It stopped him in his tracks, hitting him in the chest and snatching his breath away.

He knew it was a foolish fear. People died in all sorts of ways all the time, but that did not mean that Hetty or Noah would. He was not superstitious, he did not think there was a curse that had wiped out his family, he knew it was mere bad luck. Yet the idea of losing Hetty and Noah too was excruciating.

'Pushing them away will not help,' he reasoned with himself. They were safer with him than without, but he still felt this irrational need to hide them away, somewhere death could not find them.

Hetty turned then, perhaps sensing his presence, surprise in her eyes as she registered him.

'Richard!' she said, and he was inordinately pleased to hear her say his name again.

'Hetty.'

Noah heard his voice and spun round, running to him and throwing sandy hands around his knees. Richard lifted him up, swinging the little boy's legs out behind him, to Noah's delight.

'What are you doing on the beach so early?' Hetty asked.

'I could not sleep, and I find it impossible to lie abed if I am sure there is no chance of sleep. You are up early too.'

Hetty smiled and he was pleased to see she did not immediately make her excuses to leave. Perhaps she too had realised there had been a shift in their relationship the night before.

'Noah wakes before six every morning, sometimes even before five. He is not unhappy when he wakes, but there is no way to persuade him to go back to sleep.' She gave a little smile. 'He finds it impossible to lie abed if he is sure there is no chance of sleep.'

Richard looked down fondly at his son in his arms and wondered how much he would take after him. He looked like his brother James, but there was a hint of Hetty too about his lips and the shape of his chin. Personality would be where the familial resemblance would shine through.

Noah wriggled and Richard set him back down and the little boy resumed his game, drawing shapes in the sand with his stick.

'I am happy to stay with him if you wish to have another hour in bed.'

Shaking her head, Hetty looked over her shoulder at Noah. 'I am up now. I have to confess I do find the early mornings a challenge sometimes, but once I am up and ready for the day I do not mind.'

Their conversation was the very definition of bland, with both skirting round the intimacy they had shared the night before. Richard wondered if he should raise it, but he knew he was liable to scare Hetty off if he came on too strong. He'd promised her one night, no consequences, no expectations. Now, here he was, planning on making her his wife.

He paused. He'd shocked himself with the idea of marriage, but that was where he was hoping to end up. He did not want Hetty as his mistress; he wanted her as his wife. There would be a time in the future where they could stroll through the streets of Bamburgh arm in arm as husband and wife and it would not seem scandalous if he leaned in for a kiss. At least not too scandalous—newly married couples were granted some latitude when it came to the rules of Society.

No, he was going to have to tread carefully. His behaviour would be exemplary and he would allow her to guide the pace of their developing relationship. Of course, he hoped she would press for further intimacy, but he would work on showing her what their lives could be like if she only let herself follow her heart.

'Whilst we are alone,' Richard said quietly so Noah could not hear, 'I wanted to tell you how much I enjoyed our night together.'

She looked up sharply, as if expecting him to say more, but he just smiled at her and offered her his arm.

'Shall we take a stroll along the beach?'

Hetty was distracted as they walked along the beach. Richard had *enjoyed* their night together. On the face of it, that didn't sound that bad. At least it was a positive comment, but it was rather bland. *Enjoyable* was how you described a pleasant walk in the park or a visit to a friend's for a cup of tea and slice of cake. It wasn't how you were meant to feel after making love to the woman you had yearned for these past three years.

Since slipping from Richard's bed Hetty had been unable to think of anything else but the way his lips felt on her skin, the absolute ecstasy he induced when he touched her.

Whereas he'd described their encounter as *enjoyable*.

She tried to focus on what Richard was saying, but her mind kept slipping back to the moment he'd thrown her back on the pillows and she'd lost herself to him.

'Mr Brent and his family should be settled in their new lodgings. Perhaps we can visit them tomorrow and see how he fares after the journey. I have asked the local physician to pay a call. I am hopeful he will attend later this afternoon.'

Hetty made a little affirmative noise, her thoughts still too distracted to commit to anything else.

Richard was carrying on as if nothing had happened between them. It was what they had agreed, but it was unsettling to see him so unmoved from the encounter whereas she could think of nothing else. It had been the early hours of the morning when she had slipped from his bed and made her way back to the room she was sharing with Noah and Miss Leven and ever since she had been yearning for his touch. When he'd appeared on the beach she had thought he might suggest they allow themselves a repeat of last night, but he seemed content to stick by their agreement that it was a one-time thing only.

'He will be in need of your care these next few weeks,' Richard continued. 'But if it is too much then please do not feel under obligation to tend to him. I can look for someone else.'

'No,' she said quickly, her voice bristling with irritation. It was as if he wanted to get rid of her. First he was so dismissive of the night they'd spent together and now he was suggesting he find someone else to provide the nursing care for Mr Brent. 'I will do it.'

'Excellent. Once you have seen him, perhaps you will give me your opinion on another venture.'

'Involving Mr Brent?'

'Not exactly.'

'You are being very cryptic, my lord.' This was deliberate provocation on her part. Last night and this morning she had called him Richard, but she wanted to push him, to see if he was as indifferent about their intimacy as he seemed.

'I thought we agreed to discard any pretence of formality, Hetty,' he said. She saw a muscle in his jaw twitch and felt a slight relief. One night of intimacy had not meant he had lost interest in her.

'You wish me to call you Richard?'

'Yes. When there is no one else around.'

Hetty waited for a long ten seconds before shrugging. 'If you so desire.'

They walked on in silence and Hetty had to wonder at her own distress when she had thought Richard was now indifferent to her. She suspected he was cultivating an air of nonchalance to fulfil the promise he had made her that the night they spent together would not change anything between them.

Wondering how bold she should be to test her theory, she stopped to look back at Noah, allowing her arm to brush against him as she turned. She felt Richard tense at her touch and had to suppress a smile. He was trying hard, but proximity could make his façade of indifference falter.

Hetty should not care. She had decided there could be nothing more between them and one night together did not change that. She did not wish to become his mistress, however much she craved his touch, and she could not marry him. Richard deserved a woman who could love him fully, with the entirety of her heart, and she was not that woman. There was part of her locked away, too afraid to step into the open. She knew Richard would never hurt her, never raise his hand or force himself on her, but it didn't matter. The fear was still there, still pulsing beneath her aura of calm. It meant she had wrapped her heart in a protective layer that no one could penetrate, and therefore she could not open it up to love.

'I am considering opening a home for injured soldiers, a hospital of sorts. Somewhere they can come to recuperate and build their strength if they are discharged with wounds or injuries. A place they could receive medical attention, but more than that, a sanctuary where they can take some time to recover.'

Hetty pulled her thoughts away from how she felt about Richard to listen to what he was saying.

'Such a place would be incredible,' she said, looking at him with admiration. 'I do not think anything has been done like it before.'

'Once they had regained some physical strength there would be a focus on helping them to adapt to their injuries before they went out into the world to find work.'

'You cannot mean to employ them all as your grooms?'

Richard grimaced. 'No, I do not think my funds would stretch to that. I hope that if I can get the hospital for recovery set up, I might be able to persuade some of the other wealthy local landowners to donate. If they have invested in the early stages they might then be more willing to open their homes and their businesses to these soldiers, consider men for jobs they might otherwise pass over.'

'It is an ingenious strategy,' Hetty said. 'I think you are right. If you secure their investment in the scheme, you can slowly persuade them to help in other ways.'

'It will take time, and I am hopeful that one day it will not be needed, but even with the reduction in the size of the army since Napoleon's defeat there are still hundreds of soldiers being discharged because of injuries every month.'

'I admire your passion,' Hetty said, suddenly feeling a pang of sadness. In the past she'd had passion for her work, a drive that made her jump out of bed in the morning. The time she had spent in Portugal helping Mr Mortimer and the other surgeons had given her a sense of worth. Now she had Noah, but it would be good to feel that surge of warmth and satisfaction one could only get from a job well done, a life improved.

'Passion is one thing, but there is a long way to go to make this a reality. It may never get past the proposal stage.'

Hetty stopped, pulling away slightly, and looked up at Richard, waiting until he met her gaze before speaking. 'I think you are the most quietly ambitious man I know. Ambitious in a generous way too. You are not thinking about the best way to increase your own fortune, but you are ambitious in your plans to help others. It is commendable.'

'High praise indeed,' Richard murmured.

'I know you do not wish to have the sacrifices you have made spoken about in public, but I want you to know that I see what you do. I see what you give.'

Richard was a hard man to embarrass, but she thought she had succeeded in embarrassing him now. He swallowed and looked away and then spoke a little gruffly.

'I do not do it for the praise.'

'I know,' Hetty said, reaching out and squeezing his arm gently. 'That is what makes you even better.'

Chapter Sixteen

Mrs Wilson was a plump woman of middle age with a jolly face and strong arms that were a testament to all the manual labour she carried out. She had greeted them with enthusiasm and Hetty already felt as if she was an old friend.

'He's all settled and comfortable. The journey definitely took it out of him, but I think he has rallied a little today,' Mrs Wilson said as she ushered them through her clean and tidy hallway.

On their way into the village, Richard had told her a little of the woman who had agreed to house the Brent family and care for Mr Brent. Mrs Wilson had no formal training, but until recently had been kept busy caring for her aged and ailing parents. They had both passed away last winter and she had been left with an empty home and a lot of experience in caring for the infirm. He saw her as the perfect choice, and it sounded as though she had not taken much persuasion.

'It is a pleasure to have a child in the house, although such a skinny little boy I fear we need to build him up with some good, hearty food. He will be running around the garden in no time, I'm sure.'

'What of Mrs Brent?' Hetty asked, thinking of the malnourished, timid woman who had seemed at the end of her tether when they had visited the family in their shack.

'She has been quiet, but I think as a woman it is hard being thrust into someone else's home. I have told her she must treat it as her own and this morning she came into the kitchen to help me prepare breakfast. Sometimes a little honest labour and some companionship can cure all ills.'

Ascending the stairs, Hetty was impressed by how orderly and clean the house was. Mrs Wilson would have made a good nurse; no doubt she would have been much in demand from the surgeons, who were on the whole a messy bunch but needed a tidy environment.

They came to a stop outside a closed door and Mrs Wilson tapped gently. 'Lord Westbridge and Mrs Fairweather are here to visit,' she called breezily through the door.

There was a shuffling inside and then the door

was opened by Mrs Brent. She was wide-eyed and silent, but dipped into a curtsey as she saw Richard.

'May we come in, my dear?' Mrs Wilson asked.

Mrs Brent moved back from the door to allow them inside and then retreated to the other side of the room, where her young son was sitting and playing quietly on the floor.

'Why don't you and Thomas come downstairs for some tea and cake whilst Mrs Fairweather sees to your husband? I expect it will take a little while to dress all his wounds and I doubt Thomas wishes to see his father in distress.'

Wordlessly, Mrs Brent scooped her son up into her arms and followed the kindly older woman out of the room. Hetty and Richard were left alone with Mr Brent.

'How are you feeling after your journey?' Hetty asked, pulling up a chair to sit beside his bed. His surroundings were much more comfortable than the shack where they had seen him a few days earlier, which must help a little with the pain, but it seemed that the journey had taken its toll.

'My leg is painful,' Mr Brent said with a wince as he tried to move a little. 'And my skin feels tight.'

'The doctor came to see you yesterday, I understand?'

'Yes. He was shocked at the extent of my burns.'

Mr Brent let out a short, sharp bark of laughter. 'He said I should be dead.'

'But you are not, Mr Brent.' Hetty looked around her and saw the little vial of liquid on the bedside table. 'He has left something for the pain, I see.'

'He has, but I do not like taking it.'

'You worry you will not wake up if you drift off to sleep?'

Mr Brent nodded, tears filling his eyes. It was a fear Hetty had come across again and again whilst working close to the battlefields in Portugal. The injured soldiers always fell into two camps. The first would take any medicine offered if there was a chance of numbing the pain and the horror of what was happening to them. The second were more scared of death than the pain itself. They would force themselves to stay awake night after night, fearful that if they gave in to sleep they would never wake.

'I have two good reasons for you to take the medicine,' Hetty said, holding the man's eye. 'The first is that I am going to clean your wounds and dress them. It will be excruciating, and the medicine will dull some of that pain. To give you the best chance at survival I need to be thorough, and if you have something that will take the edge off the pain you will be able to endure more.'

'I understand,' Mr Brent said cautiously. 'What is the second reason?'

'The need for the body to heal. For you to be able to heal, to grow the new skin that is required to cover your wounds, your body needs to be rested. If you stay awake indefinitely, you will not recover. Rest is the best medicine, Mr Brent. You have to surrender to it.'

He considered Hetty's words and then nodded. 'I will take some to allow you to dress my wounds. The agony when the doctor removed the bandages was awful.'

'Good.' Hetty measured him out a spoonful of the liquid and watched him take it, and then busied herself with preparing everything she needed.

'Would you like me to stay or go?' Richard asked as she stood back and checked one final time that there was nothing missing.

'Stay. I may need your help in turning or moving Mr Brent, that is, if it is acceptable to you?' She directed the question to her patient, who was already looking more relaxed, his eyes half closed as the medication took effect.

Mr Brent waved a hand as if to say anything was acceptable to him.

Richard removed his jacket and rolled up his sleeves and Hetty took a moment to appreciate how quickly he had stepped up. She knew he was not squeamish. A man could not live through the realities of war like he had and still find the sight of blood unsettling. Nor was he afraid of a little manual labour or hard work. Still, not many earls would so willingly offer assistance in this manner.

Hetty began her work, gently peeling away the dressings and bandages to give herself an idea of what she had to deal with. There were huge areas of skin completely burned away and as she saw the extent of Mr Brent's injuries she understood why the doctor had expressed his surprise at the man still being alive. Still, there were reasons to hope too. A few areas were starting to show the first signs of healing, the edges of the wounds puckering and the fresh pink skin just starting to be visible. Also, miraculously, there were only two of the wounds that looked as if they might be infected—a victory indeed, given the lack of dressing changes and the squalid environment he had been living in the last few weeks.

She worked systematically, starting at the feet and making her way up, cleaning and applying fresh dressings, taking her time, trying to minimise the pain she inflicted.

By the time she had finished the room had grown a little darker, the sun having dropped lower in the sky. She did not know how long she had been at her work, but she thought it must have been at least a couple of hours.

'We're all done, Mr Brent.'

He let out a sigh and then reached out to grip her hand. 'Thank you.'

Inclining her head, Hetty straightened and then stretched out her back. Whilst she had been working, she had not noticed how stiff she had become, but now she needed to move, to loosen up.

'I will visit again in three days. We need to get the balance right, ensuring the wounds are clean and the dressings fresh, but allowing them to heal a little without being disturbed.'

It took a few minutes to tidy away her supplies and then she and Richard bade Mr Brent farewell.

'Thank you for your help,' Hetty said to Richard after they had said their goodbyes to Mrs Wilson and Mrs Brent and were back in the open air.

'I am happy I could be of assistance.' Richard looked pensive, and Hetty waited for him to continue. 'It has shown me how much time it can take to deal with a single patient. I must consider what staff I would need for a hospital for recuperation to deal with men who have been wounded in a similar manner to Mr Brent. You alone could not be expected to provide such care.' He waved a hand. 'That is a conversation for another time. You must be tired.'

Hetty considered. It had been a physical job, cleaning and dressing Mr Brent's wounds, but rather than feeling tired she felt invigorated. She loved the role she played in Noah's life, she would not change the time she could dedicate to him, teaching him and guiding him and playing with him, but it was also good to feel useful in another way.

She glanced at Richard and wondered if this was his intention. To give her a sense of purpose, to allow her to feel this sense of satisfaction at a job well done. She thought it probably was. He'd always been skilled at working out exactly what it was a person needed and finding a subtle way of giving it to them. It was one of the many things that had made him an excellent and well-liked senior officer in the army. Whether it was providing an extra sheet of paper for a homesick soldier to write to his family back home or knowing when to excuse a man mourning his fallen comrades from his early morning drills. He was a compassionate man, and Hetty thought he had shown that compassion towards her. He knew the sense of accomplishment her work in Portugal had given her, despite her being trapped there in difficult circumstances. In a small way, he was trying to recreate that for her here.

'You're a good man, Richard,' Hetty said quietly as he pulled away from her to open the gate that led back into the grounds of Farnleigh Hall.

Chapter Seventeen

It was the first day that had been overcast and rainy for weeks, and Richard paused before stepping out of the carriage to pull his collar around his neck. Despite the weather, he felt jubilant. Everything was coming together, he just had to keep telling himself not to rush things. His plan needed time; he would have to be patient these next few weeks.

Yesterday, Hetty had been incredible when they'd visited Mr Brent. Of course he'd seen her work in Portugal, and experienced it first-hand when she had tended to his injuries, but it was heartening to see that side of her again. Once they were in Mr Brent's room, she had taken charge with that reassuring and kind manner of hers and got the job done.

He knew she had felt a sense of satisfaction as well. He could see it in her face once Mr Brent's burns were dressed and he was lying more comfortably in bed. Nothing could boost the confidence quite like a job well done.

Today, Hetty had spent the morning with Noah whilst he had tended to important estate business, but now they were about to view the property he thought would make a good site for his proposed hospital.

Hetty was the first person he had brought here, the first person with whom he had shared the extent of his plans. Redfern knew of his desire to help wounded soldiers and assisted by directing Richard's attention to potential candidates, but he was not privy to the finer details of the scheme.

Until now, it had felt like an unobtainable dream, something he had sketched out in one of his more fanciful moments. He needed Hetty's opinion, to see if she thought his idea wildly unrealistic. If she did, he would have to return to the planning stage and start again.

'It is a good location,' Hetty said as she stepped down from the carriage and looked up at the red-brick building. 'Not far from the closest village to give you an easy supply of food and people to work in the kitchens or caring for the soldiers, but not in the centre of the village itself, affording your convalescent soldiers more privacy and space.'

'That was exactly what I thought,' he said, smiling at her.

He felt like a child on Christmas morning, the excitement bubbling up inside. It was good to have someone to share this with, to share anything with, and for the first time Richard could admit to himself how lonely he had been these last few years. He'd returned home from the army to an empty shell of a house, all the people who had once made it a home gone. Never had he shied away from his duty to the estate, but he had not been able to summon up much enthusiasm. These last few weeks, though, even the estate business did not seem so tedious, and he knew it was because he had people he wanted to share it with. Trawling through accounts and letters from his steward had once felt like such a chore, but now he viewed it as making the estate great for Hetty and Noah, for them to reap the benefits in the years to come.

'I have the keys. It has been unoccupied for some time. The last owner passed away a year ago and their son is in need of money and spends his time in London.'

Selecting the correct key from the bunch, he turned it in the lock and then opened the door.

Inside was a light and airy entrance hall with a sweeping staircase. The fact that it looked like any number of welcoming well-to-do homes was one of the things that had attracted Richard to the building. He had looked at an old orphanage and a building that had been used to house the area's poor, but they had been too depressing, too stark. Here, he could imagine men and their families finding solace, the beauty of the environment playing a part in their recovery. He did not want bare cells; he wanted functional but welcoming rooms. He did not want the dining area to replicate what they'd had in the army; he wanted these men to be able to feel human again, not like cattle.

'Tell me what you envision,' Hetty said, looking around in awe. 'For I see a house that was until recently a home, yet I think you see much more than that.'

In his excitement he forgot his plan to take things slowly with Hetty and caught her hand, pulling her with him. Hetty let out a laugh, surprised by his enthusiasm, but did not pull away.

'Imagine a grand entrance, somewhere welcoming, that pulls you into the house and sets the tone for everything else.' He led her to the left, into a room that was ideally positioned for a drawing room. 'Here we would have a social area. A place where the men could play cards and the women could write letters. Comfortable seating and a sense of normality for people whose lives have been upended.'

They moved further through, taking in the dining room, large enough to seat twenty, and continued to a room lined with bookshelves.

'This would have been the library, I presume,' Hetty said, looking a little sadly at the empty shelves.

'Yes. I thought it could be stocked again, and the room used to give lessons to the children of any of the families staying here. Just the essentials, reading, writing, arithmetic. Enough that their education is not disrupted if they normally attend school, or that they get a little basic education whilst their fathers are recuperating.'

He gripped her hand again and they retraced their steps until they were back in the grand entrance hall and heading into the east wing of the house.

'I imagined these slightly smaller rooms to be used as offices. There will need to be someone to oversee the day-to-day running of this place, to manage the finances and similar. Also someone in charge of the medical side. Any unused rooms on the ground floor could be used for storage of medical equipment.'

'You have it all worked out, don't you?' Hetty murmured as they wandered from room to room.

'I can see it all in my head,' Richard said. It felt wonderful to finally be able to share this with someone, and even better that it was Hetty. 'Shall we go upstairs?'

They made their way up the sweeping staircase to the first floor and Richard showed Hetty a series of rooms. They were similar in size and shape, some of them with dressing rooms attached. In the past they would have been the grand bedrooms of the family who owned the house, but now they were stripped bare.

'Each man would have his own room. I think it is important we give them that dignity, especially if they require treatment for their wounds.'

Hetty nodded and Richard knew she was thinking of the church where she had treated him in Portugal. There had been no real privacy there. Old pieces of fabric had been hung up to shield one group of patients from the next, but they were flimsy and did not do anything to keep out the noise, and often it was the noise that was the worst. Sometimes Richard could still hear the moans and pleas of his fellow wounded soldiers, crying out for help or for someone to end their misery.

'How would it work if the soldier brought his family?' Hetty asked, surveying one of the bedrooms with a critical eye.

'If it was just his wife, and he was not too badly injured, then she could stay in the room with him.

I think there is much to be said for the comfort that a loving companion can bring.'

Hetty looked up sharply and Richard held her gaze. He was certain he would not be alive had it not been for Hetty's care in Portugal. She had tended to his physical wounds and given him strength when his was faltering. All day he would wait for a few snatched minutes, to hear her laugh, to see the smile tug at her lips.

He made the mistake of letting his eyes flick to her lips and he felt a rush of desire. There was no furniture in the house, but he had the sudden urge to press her up against the wall and make love to her right here.

'Is something wrong?' she asked, giving him a peculiar look.

He shook his head, not trusting himself to speak. Since their night of intimacy he had barely been able to think of anything else, but he could not lose control now. Yesterday, he had seen how Hetty had glowed after tending to Mr Brent. He knew the importance of a sense of purpose, and it was just one of the things he could help her find again. Slowly, he would show her the life she could have, the sense of safety, the happiness. All he had to do was not rush things.

With great effort he suppressed the desire he felt

and continued the tour. 'If there are children then I thought perhaps a dormitory upstairs or a separate area where they can sleep with their mothers without impeding the physical recovery of their fathers.'

They finished exploring the house, taking in the smaller rooms that would once have been for the servants upstairs before heading to the kitchen.

'I wanted to show you outside...' he said, grimacing as he looked out of the window to see the heavy rain continued.

'Then show me outside,' Hetty said, this time the one to grab hold of his hand. 'It is only a little water. It will not kill us.'

Before he could protest for the sake of her health, she was pulling him up the stairs that led from the kitchen to one of the doors at the back of the house.

The ran out into the rain, their clothes immediately soaked, but all Hetty could do was turn her face to the sky and smile.

'You've lost your mind! Come, let me show you the gardens and then we can take shelter.'

They ran through a gate into the gardens proper and Richard slowed, wanting Hetty to see what he did. Here was one of the main reasons he loved this property. There were three main areas of the gardens: an overgrown formal garden, a small walled garden for vegetables and a larger open area beyond.

'This is where you would prepare these men for work,' Hetty said and he felt a rush of elation. She saw what he saw, she understood what it was he wanted to do. The streets of London and all major cities were lined with men who had once proudly signed up to fight Napoleon in the war. Sent home injured or infirm, with missing limbs and plagued by nightmares, they were denied jobs and forced onto the streets to beg. The lucky ones had families to support them, but so many were left destitute by the war and received little support from the army. It was a scandal of epic proportions, but because these men were living on the streets, dirty and often either out of their wits or drunk, no one cared, no one wanted to know the story underneath.

There was no point helping these men recover from their physical injuries if they were to be plunged straight back into poverty, no work to be found. Here, they could learn to work *with* their impediments, just as the men he employed at Farnleigh Hall had. Depending on their preference and their abilities and skill sets, they could train to be gardeners, grooms or domestic servants, learning to compensate for missing fingers or deafness or a limb injury before they went out into the world to look for work.

Hetty turned to him, her hair hanging in wet tendrils about her face, her dress sticking to her body.

'This is the place,' she said, her eyes fixed on his. 'You have such an opportunity to do good here. I think you are going to change the world, Richard.' She paused, biting her lip before continuing. 'And I would like to help you do it.'

It was exactly what he wanted to hear and he almost slipped up, almost ruined his own plan and kissed her. She looked so beautiful standing in the rain, looking up at him with eyes filled with admiration. He wondered if she was feeling more than that, if she was beginning to perhaps remember the love they had once shared. There was certainly something in the way she looked at him, but he could not assume.

He stepped back, knowing if he stood within arm's reach for a moment longer he would ruin everything with a kiss.

'I would be honoured if you would be my partner in this,' he said.

'I cannot give it what you do.'

'You do not have to. Your expertise, your experience, is just as valuable, if not more.'

'Then we shall do this together.'

Feeling his heart swell, Richard had to suppress a shout of triumph. Everything was working out exactly as he'd hoped. Hetty wanted the life he could give her, and she wanted him. He could see the desire in her eyes, could feel it in the way her touch lingered every time they were thrown together. Now, he just had to persuade her that she was worthy of it all and that she could open her heart to the love he could give her.

Chapter Eighteen

'Come with me,' Richard said as Hetty descended the stairs. He paused. 'You look beautiful, by the way.' His eyes raked over her and she felt the familiar desire well inside her. She loved the way he looked at her, as if he was tempted to throw her over his shoulder, find a private place and ravish her until she begged for mercy. As much as he tried, he could not hide his desire for her, although he had been true to his word and not once come close to acting on it. Sometimes in bed at night she wished his resolve would falter and that she would hear his footsteps outside her door, but it had not happened yet.

'Where are we going?'

'There is something I wish for you to see.'

He led her outside and onto the extensive lawn, where Noah was playing. Miss Leven was sitting a little distance away, supposedly watching over the boy, but the nursemaid looked disinterested. At first, she could not see what Noah was giggling at, but then she spotted a flash of black and a pink tongue.

'Meet Sooty,' Richard said. 'Noah chose his name. I suggested something more classical, but I was overruled.'

Sooty barked and wagged his tail and then leaped at Noah again, licking him on the face.

'That's a dog!' Hetty said, unable to believe what she was seeing.

'Your powers of observation are sharp,' Richard murmured. 'A puppy,' he corrected her. 'To grow with Noah and give him some companionship. It is not as if he will have any brothers or sisters.'

Hetty's head snapped round and she looked at Richard in surprise. She was still taken aback at the idea of a puppy. They had not discussed as yet where she and Noah were going to live in the long term. Richard seemed quite happy with them in his house at the moment, but she was aware it was not the most conventional of arrangements.

'You are forthright this evening,' she said to Richard, smiling at Miss Leven, who was listening to their conversation even though she pretended not to.

'Forgive me. Of course you may well remarry,' he said, an expression of amusement on his face. 'But courtship and marriage take time, as does the business of having a baby. Sooty can provide companionship during that time.'

Hetty sniffed. 'As you well know, I do not plan on ever remarrying,' she said. 'So you are right, Noah will not have any siblings, so praise be that you got him that dog.'

Richard leaned in closer so Miss Leven could not hear his words. 'Praise be?'

Hetty gave him a withering look and moved closer to Noah, attracting the puppy's attention. She could not deny he was adorable, a beautiful black bloodhound with a wrinkled face and oversized ears. He gave an adorable little bark and jumped up at her, licking at her hand. Hetty was smitten, although she couldn't let Richard see.

'He is irresistible, isn't he?' Richard murmured as he came up behind her.

'Sooty loves me,' Noah said, giggling helplessly as the puppy jumped onto his lap and then off again, ready to play.

'Perhaps a dog is a good idea,' Hetty conceded.

'Bloodhounds make the perfect pets. And if Noah is as keen on riding as I think he will be, he may want to train Sooty for the hunt.'

'He's two years old!' Hetty laughed, enjoying Richard's enthusiasm.

'Well, perhaps I could train him, and then Sooty would be ready when Noah is grown.'

She did not voice any of her other reservations about the idea. A dog was a commitment, if not lifelong, then at least for fifteen years or so. With the gift, Richard was showing her he expected they would still all be living together at that time. The idea was comforting and petrifying all rolled into one. Fifteen years of living here at Farnleigh Hall. Fifteen years of living and working alongside Richard. It would be wonderful, especially for Noah, but torturous as well. Having him so close but knowing they could never be together.

Then there would come the time when he would marry. No matter what he said now, he would marry, she was sure of it. He was handsome, wealthy, kind. Likely one of the most eligible bachelors in England. When he decided the time was right, he would have his pick of future bride. The idea made her feel sick. She would not be able to live here then, to watch the man she had once loved marry someone else.

She grimaced at her hypocrisy. She had always prided herself on being a kind and understanding person, yet here she was, telling Richard she did not want him but no one else could have him either.

No, she corrected herself, she hadn't told him that, but it was what she felt. She needed to make sure it did not come across in her actions. Otherwise, it was unmentionably cruel.

Fool, the voice in her head said. There was a part of her that argued almost constantly that she was doing the wrong thing. That she should grab on to Richard with both hands and never let go.

'We should leave them to it. The guests will be arriving any moment.'

'Make sure he does not go to bed too late, Miss Leven,' Hetty instructed and then went to give Noah a kiss on the head.

'I offer a thousand apologies,' Major Redfern said as Hetty entered the drawing room. He was the first of the guests to arrive and was looking distinguished in his military uniform.

'One will be enough,' Hetty said.

'I am sorry. I spoke out of turn, I was rude. I want to say I acted in the interest of my dearest friend, but Westbridge would never have spoken thus.'

It was a sincere apology and the man looked contrite.

'I accept your apology, Major. Thank you for being forthright.'

'And I thank you for your grace. Now, what do you know about our guests for the evening?'

'Nothing at all. Lord Westbridge said he was inviting a few local acquaintances. I think there will be eight of us in total.'

'Stay by my side, Mrs Fairweather, and I will guide you. Westbridge sees the good in people, but not always their less desirable side. I expect he wishes to sow the seed of the idea of investment in his charity with a few of the local landowners—that is his reason for this dinner. Well, that and introducing you to try to stem the tide of gossip sweeping the local area.'

'There is gossip?' Hetty felt a wave of panic crash over her.

'Oh, there is gossip, it would be strange if there was not. Nothing malicious, but there are many theories as to who you are and what you are doing here at Farnleigh Hall.'

'What are these theories?'

'There is, of course, the idea that you are exactly who Westbridge says you are—a distant relative fallen on hard times. Some think you are his mistress, others perhaps the mistress of one of his brothers, returned with an illegitimate son. Those who like scandalous gossip wonder if you might have been secretly married to one of the older Farnleigh brothers and your boy has a claim on the estate, they wonder whether he might legally be the Earl and you are here to negotiate Westbridge's removal.'

Raising her eyebrows, Hetty couldn't help but laugh. 'What imaginations people have.'

'There are two young women coming tonight of marriageable age, who I expect have hopes of attracting Westbridge's attention. They will be particularly interested in your role here.'

Before Hetty could enquire any more about the guests, the door to the dining room opened and Richard stepped in. He hurried over to them and clapped Redfern on the back.

'You have made amends?'

'I have apologised sincerely,' Redfern said, turning to Hetty with a smile, 'and Mrs Fairweather has gracefully forgiven me. I was just warning her about the ladies of Northumberland who are circling, looking for an opportunity to pounce.'

Richard groaned. 'You would think they would understand that a man who does not attend any of the balls or dances is signalling that he has no interest in marriage at this time.'

'They live in hope that they will be the one to change your mind,' Hetty said with a smile. 'Then it will be even more of a triumph—marriage to an earl and the story of how they were the only one able to tempt you.'

'No scheming eligible miss will be tempting me tonight,' Richard said, and then his eyes flicked to

Hetty and she felt herself grow warm from his attention. For a moment she forgot where she was and felt her body sway towards him, her eyes never leaving his.

'Good lord,' Redfern murmured. 'You cannot look at her like that when there are other people here.'

'Look at her like what?'

'Like you want to throw her over your shoulder and take her to the bedroom. Forgive my crudeness, Mrs Fairweather.'

'I did not look at her like that.'

'I know I am privy to your history, but even the most unobservant old man would be hard pressed to miss the look you two just exchanged.'

'There is nothing between us,' Richard said.

Redfern held up his hands. 'I am not here to cause any more offence. I was rude the last time I was alone with Mrs Fairweather. I promise I have your best interests at heart, but believe me when I say that others will notice it too.'

'There is nothing between us,' Richard repeated and Hetty laid a hand on his arm.

'Perhaps we should just keep our distance this evening. You can debate how historical our relationship is with Major Redfern at another time, but I think the first of your guests are arriving and we do not want them to hear us protesting our lack of feelings for one another.'

At that moment the door opened and Whitely announced the arrival of Lord and Lady Upton and their daughter, Miss Elizabeth Upton, followed quickly by Mr Eastbury and his wife and then Mr Hampton and his daughter, Miss Rebecca Hampton.

Drinks were served and introductions made. Hetty was content to stand at the edge of the room and was thankful for Major Redfern's presence at her elbow to make her seem less conspicuously separate.

Dinner was announced a few minutes later and they all filed through to the dining room. It was decorated beautifully, with dozens of candles burning around the room and the silverware sparkling on the table. She was seated next to Mr Eastbury on one side and Miss Rebecca Hampton on the other.

'It is delightful to meet you, Mrs Fairweather, the village has been fascinated by you since your dramatic arrival on that coach that overturned.'

'It was a tragedy,' Hetty murmured.

'It was. I understand you helped the little girl who injured her leg. Her mother has told anyone who will listen the kindness you showed her.'

'She had broken her leg in the accident. I helped her from the carriage and ensured the leg was splinted for the journey.'

'You are quite the practical young woman, aren't you?' Miss Hampton said, and Hetty was not sure it was entirely meant as a compliment.

'You worked as a nurse in the war,' Mr Eastbury said, joining the conversation. Hetty was glad, for she was growing uncomfortable under Miss Hampton's scrutiny.

'Yes.'

'You worked?' Miss Hampton raised her eyebrows so high they looked as though they were trying to escape her forehead.

'I did. I followed the army at the behest of my husband, and then he was badly injured and went missing in battle. I had no way home so worked as a nurse on the battlefield.'

'Fascinating,' Mr Eastbury said. 'The things you must have seen.'

'Lord Westbridge fought on the Peninsular, I understand,' Miss Hampton said, glancing up the table at their host.

'Yes, he did,' Hetty said, deciding not to feign ignorance. If she'd been a distant relative it would be something she knew about the Earl, something they had shared. 'Our paths never crossed, Portugal and Spain are vast, but I believe our time out there did overlap by a few months.'

'What a coincidence,' Miss Hampton said, and

then glanced up the table to see if she could involve Richard in their conversation. 'We are talking about your time in the army, my lord. You were in the cavalry, I understand.'

'I was, Miss Hampton. I was in the army for nearly ten years, a cavalry officer for eight of them.'

'That is where you developed your love of horses, my lord?' The question came from Miss Elizabeth Upton, who was sitting to one side of Richard. She was petite and pretty and as Hetty watched she saw her trying out her sweetest smile on the Earl.

'I rode a lot here at Farnleigh, growing up. When I joined the army, it was with the plan to become a cavalry officer.'

'What's this plan of yours to breed racehorses?' This came from Lord Upton, and Hetty could see his daughter was irritated at the interruption and Richard's attention being pulled away from her.

The conversation through dinner continued on much the same subjects. Hetty managed to bat away most questions about her life, giving vague answers until Miss Hampton grew bored and turned her attention to Richard as well. It was fascinating to see the two young women compete for his attention. He was unfalteringly polite, but at no point did he flirt or indicate he had any interest in either Miss

Hampton or Miss Upton. Both would return home disappointed tonight.

After dinner the men moved through to Richard's study and Hetty was left alone with the women as they made themselves comfortable in the drawing room. The two older women stood together talking, admiring the artwork, and Hetty found herself seated between Miss Hampton and Miss Upton.

'Do you play the piano, Mrs Fairweather?'

'No.'

'That is a shame. It is a beautiful instrument.' Miss Upton nodded over to the grand piano that sat in one corner of the room. 'I suppose when Lord Westbridge takes a wife she will likely be proficient. Men of his status do like an accomplished young woman.'

'Do you play, Miss Upton?'

'Oh, yes, I play the piano and the harp. I think it is important to bring such skills to a marriage. I can converse in French and Italian and I paint too.'

'You have had quite an education,' Hetty murmured.

'It is essential if you wish to secure an advantageous marriage,' Miss Upton said, giving a little smug smile as if she knew she would have the correct attributes.

'You are widowed, Mrs Fairweather. Tell us how you met your husband.'

Hetty swallowed, thinking back to when she'd been the same age as these young women, naïve and eager to escape her father's house.

'It is a simple story. We met when he came to visit family in the village. He was so handsome and about to embark on a career in the army. I was eager to have a home of my own, a family of my own, and when he proposed I thought he was the answer to the prayers I had been offering up.'

'Was he not?' Miss Hampton asked. It was a deeply personal question and Hetty gave a bland smile.

She had known she had made a mistake within twenty-four hours of marrying Phillip, when he had come home drunk after going out without her to celebrate their nuptials. Back then, he had not been physically violent, that had started after his stint in the army and the dishonourable discharge, but it had been clear that he was not going to be a kind and devoted husband. However, she had made her mistake and had to stick by it.

'Of course,' Hetty said with a bland smile. The last people with whom she wanted to discuss her disastrous marriage were these pampered young women who were prowling around her like wolves, trying to look for some weakness.

'You have a son too, I understand,' Miss Hampton

said. 'Everyone in the village says Lord Westbridge is very fond of him.'

'Lord Westbridge has shown us every kindness.'

'You are distant relatives? Is that right?' Miss Upton pressed now.

'Yes. Third cousins.'

'That is distant. You had no one closer to call upon?'

Hetty paused before answering and straightened, realising she did not have to subject herself to this inquisition. She had answered their questions in the hope they would cease their gossip, or at least tell their friends she was exactly what she claimed to be—a harmless distant relative whom Lord Westbridge had taken pity on, but she was not obliged to continue whilst they poked into her affairs and insinuated.

'No,' she said abruptly. 'Now, if you would excuse me, I need to check on my son. It has been lovely meeting you.' She gave an insincere smile and then rose before the two young women could say anything more.

Chapter Nineteen

The guests had all left and the house was quiet, but Hetty had slipped out anyway, seeking refuge in the garden. It was a beautiful evening and here in Northumberland the sky was dark and clear and filled with hundreds of stars.

She sat in a little gazebo, looking out and trying to suppress the sadness she felt. The dinner had been necessary, she understood that. Richard was subject to the rules of Society as much as anyone else, and he could not just move a young woman and her son into his house without expecting questions. This had allowed some of the leaders of local society to see her and meet her and understand she was not Richard's mistress, for Lord Westbridge would not be so bold as to parade his mistress at a dinner party filled with respectable people.

There had been no scandal, no questions she could not answer, but still Hetty did not feel the evening had gone well. It had shown her the difference between her world and Richard's. When it was just the two of them it didn't seem to matter that he was one of the most influential and wealthy men in England, he was just Richard. The presence of others meant she had to see him in a different light, and acknowledge that he lived in a world where she had no place.

'Was it terrible?' Richard asked as he approached the gazebo from across the lawn. He had removed his dinner jacket and cravat and rolled up his shirt sleeves. In the moonlight he looked unbelievably handsome and Hetty felt her body react.

'It was fine.'

'A ringing endorsement.'

'Miss Hampton and Miss Upton are understandably wary of me. I am living in the house of Northumberland's most eligible bachelor and I complicate their pursuit of you.'

Richard laughed. 'You make it sound like I am a poor fox and they are mounting for the hunt.'

'You joke, but that is exactly what it is like. Do you realise quite how eligible you are?'

He shrugged. 'I'm rich and titled.'

Hetty shook her head. 'I can see exactly how these women think. They have been brought up to understand their duty is to marry a wealthy, titled, well-connected gentleman. Most wealthy, titled, well-connected gentlemen are either elderly or ugly or have repugnant personalities. And then there is you. You are an attractive man, a decorated cavalry officer. You are kind, good with children and animals and you are intelligent. In short, you are exactly what they have been dreaming of since their mothers told them their whole purpose in life is to marry well.'

'You flatter me, Hetty.' He came to sit next to her, his legs brushing against hers, the heat of his body palpable even through the layer of clothes that separated them.

Turning her face up so they were only inches apart, Hetty took in everything. She knew his profile so well, from the angular jaw to the way his lips were always ready to twitch into a smile.

'No,' she said softly. 'I don't. You are the best man I know in every way. You deserve the happiest life.' And he deserved love. Hetty felt tears well in her eyes. She wanted him badly, wanted to feel his arms wrap around her, to experience the pounding of her heart as he leaned in to kiss her. She wanted to discard her doubts and give in to what they both wanted.

It would be selfish, though. She was broken. The last few years she had spent with Phillip had ruined her for anyone else. She knew what it was to love completely and unreservedly, for that was what she had felt for Richard when they were in Portugal. There had been no hesitation then. She would have followed him anywhere, made any sacrifice.

Now, she would do almost anything he asked of her, but she did not feel that same overwhelming, crashing, head-spinning love.

He deserved that.

Miss Hampton and Miss Upton were not perfectly suited to him, but there would be someone who would be. Someone who could love him as much as he deserved to be loved.

'You truly think that of me?'

She nodded, a lump forming in her throat. More than anything she wanted to kiss him, to throw away all these worries, banish all conscious thought and act on instinct instead.

Rallying, she inhaled deeply and then spoke. 'I worry about the gossip. It is clear that people are talking about us. The fact that we were on the Peninsular at the same time...'

'The arena of engagement was huge...'

'*They* have no concept of that.'

Richard shrugged. 'Let them gossip. Truly, I cannot see what harm it does.'

'It harms Noah. And it harms you.'

Richard frowned.

'If we stay here with you, the rumours that he is your illegitimate child will reach him eventually. Right now, it does not matter, he does not understand and we can shield him, but one day he will be old enough and someone will say something.'

'Then one day we tell him the truth.'

'The world is cruel to those not born legitimately.'

'I know, but I would protect him from the worst of it.'

'What about you?'

'What about me?'

'You are young and have a lot to share with the right person. You cannot marry with me living here, not if there are rumours that I am your mistress.'

'I don't want to marry someone else, Hetty.'

'You will. You will want children, a woman to share your bed, a family of your own.'

Richard fell silent, his brow furrowed, and she felt a wrench inside as she realised that she was about to lose him for good. It was the right decision, the only way to let him have a chance at the happiness she couldn't give him, but it would hurt all the same.

Richard turned to her, his knee touching hers, holding both of her hands in his.

'I don't want to marry someone else, Hetty,' he repeated, 'and the best way to protect us all from these rumours is for you and I to marry. I could adopt Noah, then there would be no gossip, nothing that could hurt him.'

Hetty felt a sudden urge to fling her arms around his neck and say *yes*. It would give her and Noah protection, a certain future, but, more than that, she would get to spend her life with Richard. There would be no reason to stay away from his bed, from his kisses, if they were married. For an instant she saw the future she could have—a life with Richard by her side, a project to fulfil her in his hospital, and perhaps more children, a little brother or sister for Noah, another child with startlingly blue eyes and a happy temperament.

It was tempting, but it would be selfish. She would be tying Richard to her and over time he would realise she could not love him as he wanted her to, as she had loved him in Portugal. Resentment would build and she would ruin this man who deserved every chance at happiness.

It wasn't even a proper proposal, just a statement of fact. If he truly believed they were right for one another he would come out with a proposal right now, but he had not. He was once again doing the right thing, taking the course of action that would protect her and Noah, whatever the consequences for him.

* * *

Richard could see she was considering the idea, but he had to tread carefully. Perhaps this was the trigger for her, seeing they were strongest when they were together, united. If she agreed to marry him, then they would be safe and settled and everything else could come later. They would have a lifetime to recover what they had lost through circumstance and bad luck, and he was sure with a few years of love and security Hetty would feel happier than she had even in Portugal.

He wanted to kiss her. She looked beautiful tonight in one of her new dresses. It was an emerald green gown, simple in design, but it complemented her colouring perfectly. There was a darker green silk sash around her waist and she wore a pair of matching green shoes. Her natural elegance and beauty meant she looked like a countess, and no doubt that was why Miss Hampton and Miss Upton had been so keen to quiz her on the nature of her relationship with Richard.

'Think on the idea. I would like to secure your future, and that of Noah's. I think this would be the best way.'

He spoke nothing of love, although his heart was brimming with it. He spoke nothing of wanting to spend every day of the rest of his life with her, and he spoke nothing of the desire that coursed through him incessantly. All of that might be too much; it might scare her away. The idea of his love for her could be slowly woven into their relationship over the next few months and years. There was no need to rush, nothing was at risk, if she agreed to marry him.

He rose, knowing that if he stayed he would say too much. Instead, he took her hand as if she were a medieval lady and he a gallant knight, and kissed her chastely on the soft skin below her knuckles.

Chapter Twenty

Hetty had not been able to rouse herself all day to do more than was absolutely necessary. The weight of Richard's suggestion sat heavily on her mind and she had been unable to think of little else. There had been moments of respite, when Noah had tempted her from her reverie with requests to play, but even then she was more distracted than she wished to be.

Although it had not been a romantic proposal, last night Richard had suggested they marry. The points he had made were not easily dismissed. By marrying him she would quieten any rumours of an illicit relationship with Richard. Instead of perpetuating the lie that she was some distant relative, they could live openly as man and wife and Richard could treat Noah as a son without too many raised eyebrows.

It might also help shield Noah against the rumours about his parentage when he was older. People might wonder at the similarity between Noah and his stepfather, especially the striking bright blue eyes, but physical similarities could be shrugged off as coincidence.

Yet, despite these very convincing advantages, Hetty knew she could not accept. Marrying Richard would be the perfect solution for her, but it would not be the right thing for him.

She felt a pang of disappointment. Although she had accepted that she would never be able to love again, she did care for Richard deeply. Being close to him made her happy. These last few weeks had been incredible and she could feel her soul healing. There was something so calming, so reassuring about his presence. He made her feel safe, but, more than that, he was helping her to discover who she was. She had been pleasantly surprised to find that she hadn't completely lost the person she once had been, and that it was possible to weave those fragments into a tapestry made up of who she was now and who she would like to be in the future.

Closing her eyes, she flopped back on her bed. Despite how she felt about Richard, she could not marry him. He lifted her up and held the promise of a better life, but she would only drag him down. The dinner party had shown her that. He was an earl, a man who was expected to marry well, but, more than that, he deserved to marry well. He deserved a wife who could stand by his side as an equal in Society but, even more importantly, a wife who could love him.

She felt tears begin to form in her eyes and blinked them away. It was no use crying; it would not change anything.

Hetty stroked Noah's hair. Tonight, she had let him climb into bed next to her and now he was sleeping peacefully, his breathing deep and even, his body still. His dark lashes rested against his rosy cheeks and she thought he looked like an angel. There would be some way through this predicament that allowed Noah to have a close relationship with his father without Hetty causing too much disruption to Richard's life. They might not be able to continue living here at Farnleigh Hall, but perhaps there was a cottage they could rent close by that would allow Richard to be part of Noah's life without Hetty hampering his chances at finding a suitable wife.

The thought of Richard finding someone else, of him pulling another woman into his arms, of welcoming her into his bed made Hetty feel sick, but she would have to get used to it. He was an eligible man, not just because of his title and fortune. Any woman would be lucky to be married to him.

'It can't be you,' she murmured to herself. Deep in her heart she knew he had to marry someone else, someone better, despite how much she yearned for him.

* * *

Richard returned home in good spirits. Everything was coming together. Today, he and Major Redfern had travelled over twenty miles to view a horse Redfern thought might be suitable for their venture into breeding racehorses. For Richard this was a secondary project, something he enjoyed and that could justify his huge stables and the number of ex-soldiers he employed as grooms. For Redfern it was a project built from passion. Together they made a good team.

The horse they had been to visit today had won a number of races but had been injured six months earlier. Initially, his owner had hoped to keep him whilst he recuperated—there was a chance he would be fit to race again soon—but pressing finances and a bank calling for sale of all assets meant he was keen to sell.

He was a beauty and they'd seen him run. Even with his injury he was fast and Richard had felt a swell of excitement as he'd watched the horse. Sometimes in life you were given a sign—a feeling he had learned not to ignore—and this was one of them. He knew this horse was going to be the perfect addition to his stables, and he'd left Redfern there to work out the details.

Richard had been eager to get back home. Normally a round trip of twenty miles would necessitate an overnight stay, but he had pushed on to Farnleigh Hall, eager to see Hetty and ascertain if she had thought any more of his offer. All day he had agonised over whether he should have proposed properly. He could have declared his love for her, promised to cherish her always, but he had wanted to tread carefully so as not to scare her off.

The house was quiet as he strode in through the front door, which was unsurprising. It was after ten and with him out for the day Hetty had probably taken advantage of a quiet evening to go to bed early. Despite Miss Leven being employed as Noah's nursemaid, Hetty was still the one who rose at five o'clock in the morning, telling Richard she cherished those early mornings with her son before anyone else was awake. He believed this was true, but he could also sense that she did not fully trust the nursemaid, especially when there was no one else up and about to keep an eye on Noah. They would have to give Miss Leven a few more days to see if she settled into the role, but she was not the nurturing, kind presence he had hoped for. Sometimes she was surly, a little abrupt with Noah, and seemed to find everything a chore. It was only fair to give her a little longer, but if things did not improve he would have to dismiss her.

Whitely hurried up the stairs from the kitchen to the entrance hall, a look of concern on his face. He took Richard's hat and helped him off with his jacket.

'Is something troubling you?' Richard asked. Whitely had been a young soldier in his own regiment, thrown from his horse at the Battle of Waterloo. Alongside an injury to his leg, he had sustained a head injury that no one had thought he would recover from. When Richard had suggested the young man come to work for him, Whitely's only request was that he never had to deal with any horses, scarred as he was from his ordeal in France. Slowly, the man was regaining his confidence. He would now ride up front in the carriage and would pet and fuss the horses in the stable, but Richard doubted the man would ever want to ride again.

'We haven't seen Mrs Fairweather all day, my lord,' Whitely said, a frown on his face. 'Miss Leven brought Noah down and I understand he has been in the nursery for his meals, but Mrs Fairweather stayed in her room.'

'Is she unwell?'

Whitely chewed his lip. 'That's the thing, my lord. Sarah went up to check on her a few times and Mrs Fairweather said she was fine and she didn't need anything, but she hasn't eaten all day and it is unusual not to see her playing with Noah.'

Richard took in the look of concern on the young footman's face and clapped him gently on the shoulder.

'Thank you,' he said. 'You have always had a keen eye for detail and kept my best interests at heart. I will go and see if there is anything troubling Mrs Fairweather.'

As he ascended the stairs he felt his heart sinking. He knew exactly what the problem was. His half-proposal the night before had been too much. These past few weeks he'd repeatedly had to remind himself to go slowly, not to do anything to spook Hetty, then last night he had wrecked everything by suggesting marriage.

Or perhaps it had been too little.

It hadn't been the least bit romantic. He'd thought to appeal to Hetty's practical side, to try to get her to see that the best way to protect her reputation and ensure Noah was shielded from any hint of scandal was for them to wed. Of course there would still be gossip, but after a few years of quiet living that would die down and Hetty would be accepted as his Countess and Noah his beloved stepson.

Hetty was a practical woman, she had been forced to be these last few years, but she also enjoyed the thrill of romance. He thought back to the occasions in Portugal where he had picked her a little posy of wildflowers or they had discussed poetry as they'd strolled along the banks of the Douro.

Before he reached Hetty's door he hesitated. It was impossible to know which way he needed to go. Did he play down the proposal from the night before, tell her they would continue to live side by side but not share any further intimacy, or did he let her know what was in his heart and hope that swayed her?

Aware that Noah might well be asleep inside, he knocked gently on the door. There was no answer and he wondered if he was overreacting. Hetty might be asleep, confused as to why he was so eager to speak to her at this time of night.

'Hetty, I'm worried. The staff haven't seen you all day.'

For a long moment there was silence and then he heard a muffled reply. 'I'm fine, Richard.'

She must have been standing on the other side of the door. Her voice was quiet, but he could sense her presence close by.

'Will you open the door, Hetty?'

At first, he thought she might refuse as for a long moment there was no movement, but then the lock clicked and the door opened.

Hetty stood just inside the room, her hair loose

down her back, contrasting sharply with the pure white of her nightgown. With difficulty, Richard did not move, suppressing the urge he had to go to her, to take her into his arms and declare his love for her.

'You've been crying.'

She shook her head. 'Only a little.'

'What has upset you so much?'

'Truly, Richard, it does not matter. You must be exhausted after your long day of riding. We can talk in the morning.'

Now he did go to her. He stepped forward and reached out tentatively to take her hand. She didn't flinch, instead curling her fingers around his and then letting out a choked sob of emotion.

'Noah is asleep in there?' Richard asked, motioning over her shoulder.

'Yes.'

'Come with me. We will be only a little way away.'

As he led her down the darkened corridor she did not resist, and before long they were settled on the cushions of the window seat at one end of the long hallway. The sun had set but the moon had not yet risen and the grounds were in darkness.

'You have been thinking of my proposal,' Richard said, not phrasing it as a question, but Hetty nodded all the same. 'Something about it has upset you.'

'I cannot marry you, Richard,' she blurted out,

pain etched on her face as she saw how the words hurt him.

For a moment he remained silent, taking in the look of distress on her face, the emotion in her voice. If he wasn't much mistaken, she wanted to marry him, but there were too many doubts, too many demons standing in her way as things were at present.

'I think you have spent the day formulating your reasons why,' he said eventually. 'Would you share them with me?'

Hetty's eyes searched his, a hint of puzzlement in them. No doubt she was wondering that he could remain so calm. What she didn't realise was that this felt like a victory. He could see she *wanted* to marry him, there was just something stopping her from accepting his proposal. He was a resourceful man. Whatever it was, he was certain they would be able to overcome it.

'You are an earl, Richard. I am the daughter of a drunkard, the widow of a scoundrel and the mother of your illegitimate son. Hardly a good candidate for Countess.'

'You would have married me, had I proposed in Portugal, before I became the Earl?'

The question seemed to throw Hetty and she didn't answer.

He batted it away with a wave of his hand. 'Is that it? Your only objection?'

'No,' she said quickly. 'Although it cannot be dismissed that easily. Last night at dinner it became woefully apparent that I am not the sort of woman you should marry. I cannot play the piano, I do not have any helpful connections, I know nothing about running a household of this size.' She stopped abruptly and shook her head. 'But that does not really matter. It would be cruel for me to marry you.' She smiled sadly and he saw the torment in her eyes.

'Why would it be cruel?'

Hetty took a deep, shuddering breath. 'I cannot love you, Richard. I doubt I will ever be able to love anyone ever again. In Portugal…' She trailed off and then seemed to rally. 'Sometimes I feel numb, emotionless. You are the best person I have ever met. You are kind and good and have the biggest heart. You deserve someone who can love you as much as you love them.'

He felt her words like a knife to the heart but managed to retain his composure. He did not believe that she was incapable of love, but he did understand how these last few years had changed her. She cared for him, she desired him, she made him happy. He did not need a declaration.

'These are your objections?'

She nodded.

'Perhaps I can address the first?'

Hetty remained silent as Richard gathered his thoughts. He'd always been skilled at debate at school and university and his clear, concise arguments had helped him to thrive in the army, yet this needed to come from the heart.

'You are right, there is a difference in social standing between us. I am an earl, I can trace my ancestors back to the time of the Norman invasion. My family has ruled over Northumberland in one way or another for centuries. Yet I am just a man. I have certain responsibilities, tenants and employees it is my duty to provide for, a place in parliament to help shape our country, but I am just a man all the same. My elevation has not changed me.'

'No,' Hetty said with a hint of a smile, 'It has not in the slightest.'

'Marriages in the upper echelons of society are made for all sorts of reasons. Money, status, access to land one family has coveted for generations. None of these are better than the others, and in most cases it breeds only resentment between a man and his wife. I do not wish for that. I would rather be married to a woman whose company I enjoy, who I can have a lively discourse with, than someone who can paint a stunning watercolour, play the piano or speak French.'

'You say that now, but what about when the other lords are looking down on you for your choice of wife, or when I make a blunder and pick up the wrong knife at a dinner party?'

Richard frowned and then laughed. 'Have you spent time with me these last few weeks? I do not wish to be friends with people who would judge someone I loved for something so superficial.' He placed his hand over hers. 'You are a respectable widow, Hetty. You would bring no dishonour to a marriage. Of course, there would be gossip for the first few months after we married, that would be the case no matter who I chose for my wife, but in a year, once people realised there was no scandal forthcoming, you would merely be my Countess.'

'You have more faith in people than I.'

'I have led a more privileged life than you, but I honestly believe people would soon find more interesting things to gossip about than our marriage.'

Hetty chewed her lip and he could see his calm argument had swayed her on this point at least.

Impulsively, he reached out and cupped her cheek, waiting for her to raise her eyes to meet his before he moved closer. Gently, he kissed her, revelling in the sweetness of her lips. Part of him wanted to declare his love now, to tell her he adored her, that he would do anything for her, but he knew he had to tread carefully. For tonight, this was enough.

'Get some sleep,' he said softly. 'Tomorrow, I wonder if you will take a walk with me in the grounds? We can talk more then.'

It would be harder to sway her when it came to her second objection, but he had an idea what might work. Sometimes there was nothing quite like a grand gesture.

Chapter Twenty-One

'Shall we take a stroll?' Richard offered her his arm and Hetty took it without hesitation. She had slept more soundly the night before and this morning had woken with a peculiar sense of anticipation and hope. Richard might have persuaded her that the difference in their class did not matter, but there was still the enormous issue that she did not want to tie him to a woman who could not love him as he deserved.

They walked through the gardens, heading out into the wider grounds towards the lake. At first Richard remained silent, but Hetty could sense a tension beneath his outward demeanour of calm.

'Can I ask a favour of you, Hetty?'

'Of course. Anything.'

'I ask that you carefully consider what I say this next half an hour. Any decisions you make are your own, but please do not make up your mind before you have heard what I have to say.'

'I can do that.'

'Wonderful. Then would you care to step into the boat?'

They had reached the lake and bobbing at the shore was a little weatherbeaten rowing boat.

Hetty frowned. This was not what she had expected at all. She had thought Richard would sit her down and list all the reasons it made sense for her and Noah to stay here at Farnleigh Hall. Instead, he was taking her out on a trip across the lake.

Once she was settled on one of the benches, Richard pushed the boat off from the shore, hopped in and took his position in the middle, using both oars in tandem to pull them through the water. He had considerable upper body strength and they flew across the calm surface as if propelled by one of the mechanical engines she had read about in the newspaper.

Hetty wondered if Richard rowed regularly; it would be one way of keeping his body in such peak physical condition, and the ease with which he manouevred the boat made her think he must do this more than once or twice a year.

'There is a little island in the middle of the lake. When I was a boy, my eldest brother, George, taught me to swim by asking our cook to bake my favourite cake. He rowed it out to the island and then told me I could have it all if I swam out.'

'Did you make it?'

'Yes. Although I do not know how I survived. I must have swallowed half the lake water on the way. I was so sick when I finally pulled myself to shore that I wasn't able to have any of the cake anyway. My brothers kindly ate it for me.'

'Siblings can be a blessing and a curse all rolled into one, I suppose,' Hetty said with a smile. She had always wished for a sister, someone to confide in and share her troubles with, but her parents never had any more children.

'It did the job though. After that, I wasn't afraid of the water and soon I picked up the technique that allowed me to make it across the lake without imbibing anywhere near as much.' He smiled. 'We are going to that little island now, although I will not make you swim.'

'Thank goodness,' Hetty said. She had mastered many skills in her lifetime, but swimming was not one. The part of Essex she came from was landlocked and she had never fancied jumping into the rivers and ponds near her childhood home. It meant that she now had a mild fear of being submerged in water, which had become most apparent when she had travelled back by ship from Portugal.

As they approached the island, Richard jumped out as the boat hit the sand and pulled it up onto the beach. Once he was satisfied that it was not going to float away, he reached in and helped her to her feet.

Hetty saw that a little distance away a blanket had been laid out and a basket was set upon it.

'You've brought me for a picnic?' she asked, surprised.

'I have. A picnic with one of my favourite views in the world.'

She turned and her breath caught. In the foreground the water sparkled and shimmered, whilst beyond there were the greens and yellows of the rolling hills. Perched in the middle, framed perfectly, was Farnleigh Hall.

Richard ensured she was settled and comfortable before picking up the bottle of champagne and opening it.

'I thought champagne was for celebrations,' Hetty said.

'I have much to celebrate.'

He handed her a glass and then sat down beside her, raising his glass in the air in a silent toast before bringing it to his lips. She followed, enjoying the sweet taste and the bubbles that made her tongue fizz. Richard looked nervous and shifted position a few times before beginning to speak. It was unusual for him not to be confident and self-assured.

'A month ago, I was lonely, wallowing in self-pity, unable to summon the enthusiasm to properly take care of the estate. I had my projects—the idea of the hospital, the scheme to help injured soldiers find work, the building of a stable of racehorses that will one day go on to win national acclaim—but I was drifting through life, feeling disconnected, ungrounded.' He paused, looking up at her. 'Then you arrived, bringing Noah into my life and, alongside Noah, you.'

'It must have been quite the shock.'

'It was the shock I needed. I have lost many people I loved, both at home and whilst serving in the army, but I am still alive. I think I needed to be reminded of that.'

'I think I know what you mean,' Hetty said quietly. 'I never thought I would feel enjoyment again, happiness, but being here, with you, the fear and pain started to melt away.'

Her contribution seemed to spur Richard on. He was looking out into the distance, his eyes fixed on the outline of Farnleigh Hall.

'I sometimes worry that I am going to lose everything I care about. I think it is one of the many reasons I felt I could not become invested in the estate here at Farnleigh Hall. I thought if I cared about it, I would lose it.'

'That is understandable, given what has happened these last few years.'

'I have been doing a lot of thinking these past few days and I realised how lucky I am, and that it was fine to *feel* lucky. It does not invalidate my sadness at the deaths of my brothers to appreciate what I have now.'

Hetty nodded. She could understand the complex path his emotions were treading. The guilt he must feel when he realised that he was living the life his eldest brother should have had.

'I am lucky because I have a wonderful home, and enough money that I think I can do some real good in the world. I cannot help every soldier that is injured from the army, but I can change the lives of some. That sense of purpose is not to be underestimated. I have a wonderful son—' he paused and reached out and took Hetty's hand '—and the woman I love is alive and well.'

Hetty inhaled sharply, her eyes searching his face for an answer. It was the first time he had said he loved her and she hadn't realised how much the words mattered. He showed it in the things he did for her, the way he always ensured she was cared for and comfortable, but he hadn't said the words before. She wished more than anything she could say it back to him.

'I love you, Hetty. I do not think I made that clear when we were sitting in the gazebo. I was too afraid of scaring you off, but it is important you know how I feel before you make any decision about your future.'

'Richard, I...'

'Please, Hetty. I do know your objections, but please let me say what I need to.'

She nodded and waited for him to continue.

'I loved you in Portugal. I loved you when I thought you were dead and I love you now. That love has changed and developed, but it is love.'

They had shared so much, and through it all he had loved her. For a moment she felt a hot flash of anger at the injustice of the world. After their initial wonderful few weeks together they'd been ripped apart. If they hadn't been separated, then everything would be different.

'Now, here is the important part. I know you have had a truly terrible few years. I cannot begin to imagine what it does to a person to be threatened and belittled and abused by someone who is meant to love and cherish you. I can understand your emotions changing, even your sense of self changing. And I hear you when you say you cannot love me.' He paused, holding her gaze in a bid to make sure she knew he was sincere. 'I know you care for me, and I have thought long and hard about this. For me, that is enough.'

Hetty let out a little sob, her emotions too big to be contained within her body. His words were the most generous thing anyone had ever said or done for her. To let her know that he still loved her, even though she could not return that love in full… Hetty felt her heart pound in her chest and she couldn't finish the thought. It was monumental and on hearing his words it felt as if the whole world had shifted.

'Do not think I delude myself, that I think one day you will learn to love again. Of course, I would be thrilled if that did happen, but I am perfectly happy if this is what we share. Affection, attraction, a mutual respect. It is a lot more than most marriages are built upon.'

'You deserve more than that. You deserve a woman who can love you as fully as you love them.'

'What I want, from the bottom of my heart, is you, Hetty.'

He reached out and traced the curve of her cheek and she was reminded that he had already helped her to heal so much. A few weeks earlier she could not bear to be touched, could not bear for anyone but Noah to come close. Every interaction she had greeted with fear, yet Richard, with his patience and his gentleness, had slowly helped her to recover. Now she yearned for his touch. There was no fear as his fingers gently stroked her cheek, no concern that the caress might turn into a slap or his fingers might drift south to close around her neck.

'I am going to ask you a question now, but I do not want you to answer it yet. I will respect whatever answer you give me. I give you my vow that I will not press you again, but please take a few hours, a day even, to make your decision.'

'I will,' Hetty said and she turned to face him fully, her heart fluttering.

'Hetty, I love you. I can give you a comfortable life, a happy home for our son, and I promise I will always keep you safe. Will you marry me?'

It was a wonderful proposal, and for the first time Hetty realised she might be able to say yes. Sitting here with Richard, she felt at peace, happier than she had thought possible a few weeks earlier. Last night she had been confused and upset and Richard had gently coaxed her worries from her. Instead of responding with anger, he had calmly laid out why he disagreed with her, and even his proposal was done in such a way that did not put any undue pressure on her. He made her feel loved and he made her feel safe.

She would take the time to consider his proposal. If they did marry she wanted to be sure it was the right decision for Richard, but in her heart she already knew what her answer would be.

He pressed a finger to her lips. 'You will consider everything I have said before you give your answer?'

'I will, Richard.'

'Thank you, that is all I ask.'

She felt an overwhelming affection for him. He was the absolute opposite of her late husband, calm and patient and considerate.

With a gentle hand, she reached out for him, running her fingers through his hair, and then, ever so slowly, she rose up on her knees. She wanted to show Richard how much he meant to her, how she had never thought she would want to be intimate with anyone again but within a few short weeks he had her thinking of little else. There was a look of surprise on his face as she kissed him and then, with a firm but gentle hand on his chest, she pushed him back onto the blanket.

She straddled him, having to pause a moment as her dress got caught underneath her, and then she lowered her hips onto his. They were both still fully clothed but the movement was sensuous and Hetty felt Richard harden beneath her.

She kissed him, a long and leisurely kiss, enjoying the idea that they had all the time in the world. If they married they could do this every single day, and the idea excited her. Gently, she slipped her hand into the waistband of Richard's trousers and deftly she unfastened them, all the time her hips rocking gently back and forth, creating a wonderful warmth between them.

'Hetty,' he murmured, his hands tangling in her hair, tugging at the pins that held her low bun in place to release her hair so it flowed over her shoulders.

He groaned as her hand brushed against his hardness and she revelled in the power she held over him as she gripped his manhood fully, holding it for long agonising seconds before she started moving her wrist up and down. His desire for her was intoxicating, especially when Hetty felt the same for him.

As Richard's head fell back, his breathing heavy with desire, Hetty adjusted her undergarments and positioned herself above him and then, with a sigh of pleasure, she lowered her hips to meet his.

He gripped her at the waist, thrusting up inside her, but Hetty pressed down firmly, not allowing him to move. Only when he released her did she start again, lifting and lowering herself rhythmically but oh, so slowly.

He let her control the pace, the expression on his face one of pure happiness. Hetty's head dropped back, her breath came faster and she let out a little moan as she felt the tension begin to build. Then her climax crashed over her and she felt herself clench around Richard, all sense lost as she abandoned herself to pleasure.

Afterwards, Richard put his arms around her and pulled her onto his chest and Hetty marvelled at the peace and happiness she felt. A few short weeks ago, such emotions had felt completely out of reach.

She wondered if she should give him her answer now, but he had asked her to give it proper consideration so that was what she would do. Perhaps this afternoon she would be able to call him her fiancé. The thought sent a thrill of joy through her and she held him a little tighter, hoping he could sense her contentment.

Chapter Twenty-Two

They walked hand in hand across the grass, their pace leisurely. Hetty brought her hand up to check her hair. It was always difficult to pin it neatly without a brush or mirror, but Richard had assured her she looked presentable.

She was in shock, surprised at herself and at Richard. Never had she expected to be persuaded by him that their life together could be a happy one. She had become so fixated on this idea that she could not love him as he deserved, she had not thought about what it was he wanted, or indeed what she could bring to him. For so long she had thought of herself in a negative way. There were only so many times you could be called a burden and a disgrace before you started believing it, even if you knew the man saying those things to be cruel.

Richard was right though. They could share a

happy union even if her heart was damaged, unable to love as it should.

She felt a thrill of happiness when she thought of Noah and the life he would have now too. When she married Richard, Noah would be his stepson but there would be no eyebrows raised if he went through the process of adopting Noah, making him his legitimate heir. It would mean that their son would always have a place in the world and a father who loved him.

Of course there were still niggling doubts in her mind, but she had seen the sincerity in Richard's eyes and she had believed him when he said he would choose her and whatever form her affection for him took in preference to anyone else.

When they reached the house, one of the maids told them that Noah had wanted to go to the stables and a reluctant Miss Leven had taken him.

'I think we need to find a new nursemaid,' Hetty said, biting her lip. She liked giving people a chance, but there was something she didn't like about Miss Leven. Perhaps it all stemmed from the incident at Dunstanburgh Castle, where she had not been quick enough to respond, but Hetty didn't think it was just that. Miss Leven did what was required, but sometimes she seemed a little short with Noah, a little irritated. It was difficult looking after a small child, but that was Miss Leven's entire role here at Farnleigh Hall and she had hardly embraced it.

'I agree, she is a little sour, is she not?' Richard said. They were still walking slowly, still in the blissful haze after their intimacy on the little beach.

'We need someone trustworthy, reliable, someone who loves Noah almost as much as we do. Especially if I am to help you with your hospital.'

'Yes, there will be many demands on your time,' he said, his lips close to her ear.

As they walked into the stable yard there was no sign of Noah, but Miss Leven stood talking to one of the grooms. She was leaning towards him, a coy smile on her face, twiddling a loose strand of hair around her finger.

'Are the horses all exercised for the day, Jones?' Richard called out good-naturedly to the groom, who quickly doffed his hat and hurried away.

Miss Leven turned, pouting, but didn't say anything.

'Where is Noah?' Hetty said, a note of panic audible in her voice.

'He's in the stable, looking at the horses, Mrs Fairweather.'

Hetty felt Richard stiffen beside her and then he took off at a run. She followed, hoping they would find him sitting on one of the bales of hay or admiring the horses from outside the stalls.

As Hetty reached the entrance to the stables her heart jumped into her throat. Noah was hanging over the barrier that separated the main part of the stable from one of the horse's stalls. He'd pulled a nearby block of hay over to stand on to get a better view of the horse, but now he was teetering unsteadily on it. The horse behind the barrier was huge, a great dark brown stallion, stamping its hoof at the intrusion into its space. Noah, unaware of the danger he was putting himself in, continued to swing on the barrier.

It was as if the world had slowed for Hetty as she watched Noah lean too far and topple over into the stall. Richard was already running, his feet pounding on the flagstones, but he was still too far away. If the horse reared up in fright its hooves could crush Noah's delicate skull in seconds.

Hetty felt her whole world implode as panic overtook her. She could not tear her eyes away as the horse whinnied and then reared up on its hind legs. Noah lay beneath him, helpless, in the hay.

Richard scooped up Noah's tiny body a fraction of a second before the hooves came thundering down. Noah screamed, pure fear in the sound, but Richard had him now and was holding him close to his chest.

Hetty finally could start moving again and she

rushed to Noah, taking him from Richard's chest and holding him to her own. Their son sobbed, burrowing in to her, and she held him tightly.

For a long moment Richard stood there, his arm around Hetty's shoulders, his focus entirely on their son. Only when Noah's sobs reduced did he look away. At first Hetty did not understand the transformation that Richard underwent. One instant he was the concerned father, comforting the woman and child he loved, the next he was like a man possessed. He stormed down the length of the stables, his face red with anger, his fists clenched by his sides. He didn't stop until he was towering over Miss Leven, inches away from her. The young woman cowered under his glare.

Hetty felt a rush of panic. There was something about the pure anger in Richard's expression that took her back to the tiny house in Essex. She felt her pulse quicken, her heart start to pound in her chest. The edges of her vision went blurred and grey and she blinked rapidly, trying to clear it. Her hearing was muffled as if she were trying to listen to something underwater.

In front of her, she saw Richard transform into someone else, his eyes had turned darker, his face not his own. She could see his hands were shaking and were clenching into fists and unclenching.

She stumbled back, trying to get away, convinced that Phillip was about to appear and put his hand around her neck and try to squeeze the life out of her. Somewhere in her rational mind she registered that Richard did not touch Miss Leven, but he did shout. He asked her if she was deliberately trying to kill his son, given this event and the one on the clifftop at Dunstanburgh Castle.

Hetty did not hear what Miss Leven said in response, but Richard let out a grunt of disdain and told her to pack her bags and leave Farnleigh Hall immediately. After the nursemaid turned to leave, Richard let out a feral growl and then smashed his fist into the wall.

Clutching Noah tight to her, Hetty began to back away further. She was not in control of her mind or her body, pure panic pulsing through her veins. She wanted to run, to tell Noah to hold onto her neck, and leave as quickly as possible.

Recognising this was not a rational response, Hetty tried to breathe deeply, tried to regain some of her sense, but it was impossible. Her body started to shake and as Richard turned and stepped towards her, she felt irrational fear.

He was shaking as he moved towards her, his hands trembling and his eyes unfocused. His fingers were bleeding from where he had struck the wall, but he didn't seem to notice. It was as if he wasn't actually there at all.

With great effort he seemed to drag himself back from wherever he had gone. It took a long moment for the darkness to lift, for his face to return to normal, and even in her distress she could see the effort it cost him.

'Hetty? What is wrong?'

He moved quickly now, arriving at her side within a few seconds, but she could not stand his proximity, could not bear it when he reached out and placed a hand on her shoulder, even though he was so gentle.

'Get off...' she managed to gasp, and despite the panic she felt she registered his wounded expression. *This* was what she had been afraid of, that the damage she had sustained in her past, invisible but always bubbling under the surface, would affect him.

She backed away, tears falling onto her cheeks.

'Hetty, I don't understand. Noah is safe, he is unharmed. Between us, we will ensure he is never put in harm's way in this manner again.'

With a gasping breath she shook her head, motioning for him to stay back when he reached out. Again there was the pained expression, and with a breaking heart Hetty knew what needed to be done.

'I can't marry you,' she said, the words coming out in a strained rasp. She felt her heart crack in two as soon as she had said it and turned before she could see the devastation she had wreaked.

Clutching Noah tightly, she ran as well as she could with the little two-and-a-half-year-old attached to her neck. She headed for the house, knowing she needed solitude, to get away from Farnleigh Hall. She would have to leave, to put physical distance between them and go somewhere Richard could not follow her, as right now she could not deal with his heartbreak alongside her own.

Chapter Twenty-Three

'Hurry, Noah,' Hetty said, throwing the last of their meagre possessions into a bag and fastening it. It was the coward's way out to flee, but she needed some space and time to get her thoughts straight, and she would not have that if she stayed here at Farnleigh Hall. Richard would be concerned, of course he would, but once they were settled elsewhere she could send him a letter explaining everything.

Hetty felt the weight of her decision pressing on her shoulders and had to force herself to be strong. She still felt the panic she had in the stables, the raw fear coursing through her veins. She needed time to work out what that meant for her future.

'It has to be done,' Hetty reassured herself. Their situation was too complex, too messy. Whilst she was living here under his roof, neither of them could think straight.

'I don't want to go,' Noah said, crossing his arms

and sitting down on the floor, a frown fixed upon his face. She had not told him they were leaving for good, but no doubt he had sensed her upset, her frantic packing. Even at two-and-a-half he could see that something was going on that he would not like.

'It is just a trip to Bamburgh. I will find us a lovely little room to stay in.' She bit her lip guiltily. Still, she did not have any money of her own. These last few weeks Richard had paid for everything. From tomorrow she would set about finding some work, but she would have to secure the room with a promise that Richard would pay for it. It was not ideal and she cursed herself for being swept up in a sense of comfort and security these last few weeks.

'Sooty come too,' Noah said, his chubby little arms crossed in front of his body.

'No, Sooty wants to stay here and play in the garden. We can come and visit him soon.'

'No Sooty. No Noah.'

Hetty sighed and slumped down onto the floor beside her son, holding out her arms until he relented and climbed into her lap.

For a few minutes she sat holding him, not moving. She inhaled the scent of his hair, felt the warmth and weight of his body in her arms. It was a familiar feeling, and it grounded her. Inside her chest, her heartbeat slowed and her breathing became steadier, more rhythmic. Some of the panic that had filled her in the stables was starting to subside, but still her mind felt overwhelmed.

'It is an adventure,' she whispered to Noah. 'Noah and Mama, going on an adventure, just like the one we went on to get here.'

'I don't want any more adventures.' It took him three attempts to get the word adventure out, but when he did Hetty felt as if she had received a blow to the stomach. With this move she was wrenching Noah from the first place he had felt safe and taking him elsewhere, to another unknown room.

This time when she stood, Noah stood with her, slipping his hand into hers. She picked up her bag and with one final glance over her shoulder they left.

Hetty felt uncertain as she and Noah crept out of the front door, but she forced herself to keep walking. They had survived much worse than this, although none of that had been self-inflicted.

'Room and board is included in the price. You'll get your breakfast and dinner, but only if you are here at six o'clock sharp.'

'That is not a problem,' Hetty said, looking round the small room with a critical eye. It was clean, that was her main criteria when she had started her search for somewhere for her and Noah to stay. There was a bed big enough for both of them, made up with fresh sheets and blankets, and after the long walk to get here, much of it carrying Noah, she wanted nothing more than to collapse into it.

'You say Lord Westbridge will settle the bill?' the woman asked, looking Hetty up and down sceptically.

'Yes. He will pay for the first week straight away and then on a week by week basis ongoing.'

Hetty suppressed a swell of panic at the idea of living in just a single room with Noah. After the luxuries of Farnleigh Hall it would be difficult to adapt. Here there was no garden, no servants to watch him whilst she went to the toilet or got herself dressed. Of course they had lived like this before, and their interlude at Farnleigh Hall had been short, but it was surprising how quickly she'd got used to those things.

The landlady gave a nod of satisfaction. Apparently, despite only arriving in Northumberland a few weeks earlier, she was well enough known that the landlady trusted Hetty was who she said she was. She wondered what it must be like to be under this sort of scrutiny your entire life. It didn't seem to bother Richard, he rose above the gossip as if it couldn't touch him, but she knew that rumours could destroy even the most influential of men.

Noah looked around miserably, his bottom lip pouting. 'I want to go home.'

'This will be our home for the next few weeks,' Hetty said, trying to make her voice as cheerful as possible. 'Look, there is one lovely bed for me and you to share.' Normally, he wanted to snuggle up with her at night, so it was telling that even this couldn't rouse a smile. She picked him up and cuddled him, trying to convince herself she wasn't a bad mother. She could give him everything he needed right here. Hundreds of thousands of families lived in conditions such as these and raised their children perfectly well.

'I want Sooty.'

'We will go and visit Sooty soon.'

'I want Richard.' This was said in a quiet voice and when Hetty looked down she could see tears in her son's eyes.

'I know,' she said, kissing the top of his head. Right now, she wanted Richard too. She wanted him to burst in through the door and gather them up into his arms, insisting they come home with him.

Rubbing her forehead with her free hand, she tried to stave off the headache that was brewing. Some distance from Farnleigh Hall and from Richard was a good thing. Already her thoughts felt a little clearer, her panic at Richard's reaction to Miss Leven was settling. Now, she just had to work out what it meant for their future.

Chapter Twenty-Four

It had been twenty-four hours since Hetty had declined his proposal and Richard still felt as though he had been punched in the gut. Initially, he had tried to follow her, but she had shut him out, refusing to open the door to her bedroom. He'd heard her in there crying, but there had been nothing he could do. Then she had disappeared—taken Noah and fled Farnleigh Hall as if she was frightened for her life.

He felt sick at the idea that he had scared her. These last few weeks, the lasting impact of the abuse she'd received at the hands of her husband had become devastatingly apparent and he had done everything he could to ensure she felt safe here with him. Then he had destroyed it all with one angry outburst.

Now he felt numb. When they'd been on the little island in the middle of the lake he had been sure she was going to accept his proposal. She had seemed so happy as they'd walked back to find Noah, and now she had fled Farnleigh Hall in fear of what he might do.

Swinging the axe, he split the wood in perfect halves, throwing them both on the ever-growing pile of chopped logs for the fire. Sweat trickled down his back and in his frustration he pulled his shirt over his head and threw it to rest onto a fencepost nearby.

Without pausing to catch his breath, he selected another log and began the process of splitting it. What he wanted was to fight someone. In the army there had been plenty of young soldiers who boxed. They would set up makeshift boxing rings and take bets and then the young men would pummel each other until one man was too dazed to pick himself up from the floor. Richard had never seen the appeal, until now. He would relish a fist to the face, revel in the feeling of the skin of his knuckles splitting as he hit back. Alas, there was no one to fight, no one to take his frustration out on, so instead he continued with the axe and the ever-dwindling pile of logs.

The thought of violence made him pause. *That* was the problem. When Noah had fallen into the horse's stall, almost to be crushed by the hooves of an animal many times larger and stronger than himself, Richard had felt pure panic. It was only when his son was safe that the panic had turned into something much darker.

He knew that what he had seen in the war still affected him. Every so often he had awful nightmares, dreams where he saw men he considered friends slaughtered, where he discovered the atrocities that had been brought upon the local people for helping the English. The dreams had been more frequent when he'd first left the army, but he doubted they would ever really leave him.

There was more to it than dreams though. Sometimes something innocuous would trigger him and for a moment he would find himself back in the midst of battle. He would hear the thundering of the horses' hooves and the cannon and smell the terrible mixture of blood and grime. His heart would pound and he would get a surge of aggression and fear and it would be as if he were charging into battle.

That was what had happened when he had realised the danger Noah had been in. His reaction had been severe, although he'd been in control enough not to lay a finger on Miss Leven. Even so, he could see why it had scared Hetty so much. Hetty, who had spent the last few years cowed, living in fear, never knowing when her late husband might erupt into violence.

With a growl of frustration, he swung the axe again. He'd driven Hetty away with his reaction, and it was all his fault.

'Is it safe to approach?' Redfern called from a good distance away.

Richard paused, hefting the axe over his shoulder and taking a step back from the woodpile. He nodded, his chest heaving with the exertion.

Redfern looked at the sizeable pile of chopped wood to the left of the block and raised an eyebrow. 'You have been at this quite some time. Has it made you feel better?'

'No.'

'Then perhaps it is time to stop and come drink some of that excellent whisky you have in your study.'

Richard contemplated the suggestion for a moment before swinging the axe a final time and burying the tip in the chopping block.

'And good lord, man, put on a shirt. No one needs to see *this*, it makes a man feel ashamed.' He motioned to Richard's physique and for the first time in twenty-four hours Richard smiled.

'Tell me,' Redfern said a few minutes later as they sat in Richard's study, both with a glass of whisky in hand.

'Hetty has taken Noah to Bamburgh. They've rented a room.' One of the servants had heard the news in the village and informed him earlier that morning. He was glad that Hetty and Noah were safe, and not too far away, but he hated that he had driven them from Farnleigh Hall.

'Peculiar. Did she give a reason?'

Richard groaned, wondering how he could explain what had happened in the stables.

'Miss Leven, Noah's nursemaid, put him in danger. I reacted badly. I shouted at the woman and punched the wall once she had left.'

Redfern cocked his head to one side. 'A relatively extreme reaction, but if the nursemaid had put Noah in danger...' He trailed off and gave a shrug.

'Hetty's husband hurt her. She hasn't told me the details, but I think he hurt her in every way possible. When she first arrived here she couldn't even bear to be touched for the most innocuous of reasons.'

'Ah. Some men are brutes.'

'They are, and I think Mr Fairweather was one of the worst.'

The two men sat in silence for a minute, the only noise Redfern's fingers as he tapped on the arm of his chair.

'The worst part about it is that it is all my fault,' Richard said, throwing back the whisky and topping up both glasses. The liquid burned as it hit the back of his throat, before the burn settled to a satisfying warmth.

Redfern raised an eyebrow but did not interrupt. He was a man who knew how to listen.

It took Richard a few minutes to collect his thoughts before he said anything more. It felt odd to be speaking out loud what he had kept secret for so long.

'Sometimes I lose control,' he said quietly. 'Not often now, but when I do it comes without warning. There is always a trigger—a loud noise or a stressful situation—but I swear when it happens it feels as though I am back on the battlefield.'

He glanced over at his friend and saw Redfern was clutching the arms of his chair, uncharacteristically on edge. He wondered if he had shared too much.

'I too have experienced this,' Redfern said eventually. 'And on speaking to many of the soldiers who have returned from Europe, those who were at the worst skirmishes and the bloodiest battles often describe something similar.'

'I did not know,' Richard said, wondering if he should have seen any sign that his friend was suffering too.

'I do not like to talk about it.' Redfern shrugged and then glanced over at Richard. 'Do you have the dreams too?'

'Yes. More vivid than any dream I have ever had before.'

'It is as if I am back there, seeing the bodies fall

all over again.' Redfern shook his head, seeming to rouse himself. 'Enough about me. Have you told Hetty about this?'

'No.'

'So she doesn't know why your reaction was so strong.'

'No.'

'I have no experience in matters of the heart,' Redfern said slowly. 'All I know is the military. In the army, if faced with difficulties it is advised to disseminate information to the key players. Commanders cannot decide what is best without knowing what they are fighting. I think you owe it to Mrs Fairweather to give all the available information before she makes a final decision.'

Richard nodded. As always, his friend spoke sense. Yet he felt a deep dread at having to put into words the uncontrollable emotions that rolled over him when one of these episodes happened.

If she rejected him when she had all the information then… He grimaced. Then he would have to accept her decision, but perhaps right now there was a glimmer of hope.

'Wait a moment longer,' Redfern said, resting a hand on Richard's shoulder. No doubt he had seen the determination in his friend's eyes and knew Richard was planning on rushing into Bamburgh now. 'She has said she is not going anywhere as yet. You have time, I suggest you make a plan rather than dashing madly in.'

Sinking back into the chair, Richard nodded in agreement. Redfern spoke sense. If he turned up now, his breath heavy with whisky, his emotions out of control, no doubt he would remind Hetty again of her late husband. That was the last thing he needed. Instead, he must pause, to think this through logically.

Letting out a groan of frustration, he thumped the arm of the chair. 'In all things I can see the rational path, I know instinctively what to do next. Yet with this I feel as though I am lost in the darkness.'

'It is because you care so much. It is no bad thing. Take a moment. What is important to Mrs Fairweather?'

'Noah,' Richard answered quickly.

'Good. What else?'

'Safety, security, somewhere she does not have to live in fear.'

'Anything else?'

Richard considered and was surprised with his next answer. 'Me.'

Redfern looked at him in surprise, but motioned for him to continue.

'She cares for me. I do not think that will have

changed, but I scared her and she will be doubting whether she can trust me, wondering if I would hurt her.' Even the idea of ever hurting Hetty, even accidentally, made him feel sick and he hated that he might ever make her feel that way.

Richard stood and placed his whisky glass on the table. An idea of what he might say to her was beginning to form and he felt a glimmer of hope. He could not know the outcome, but he owed it to himself to do the very best he could. If she refused him, then at least he would know it was not because he had not tried.

Chapter Twenty-Five

Hetty struggled to get out of bed the next morning. Noah was playing quietly in one corner of the room and she was thankful that he seemed more settled this morning.

The previous day had been difficult. Noah had asked seemingly a hundred times to return to Farnleigh Hall, wanting to see his puppy, to see Richard, and to sleep in his bed in the nursery. Hetty had gritted her teeth and kept her patience, knowing it was her fault her son was so unsettled. She had held him close as he'd drifted off to sleep the night before and it had broken her heart to hear him whimper and then whisper Richard's name.

Today she was due to see Mr Brent. She did not have the bag of supplies, but she hoped it might have been left at the property for her. Wherever the bag was, she planned to call on Mr Brent anyway, to see how he fared. If there were no clean dressings available she would ask Mrs Wilson, the widow taking care of the ex-soldier's day-to-day needs, if she could arrange for it to be fetched.

She sighed, finally rising and starting the process of washing and getting dressed. Her whole body felt heavy, as if it did not belong to her, and that was partly because she had slept so badly. Most of the night she had lain awake, careful not to toss and turn but still uncomfortable, thinking about the day before.

Richard's reaction to Miss Leven's carelessness had been extreme, but perhaps not completely unwarranted. It was the second time the nursemaid had put Noah in danger with her neglect, and both times it was only Richard's quick thinking that had saved their son. He had a right to be angry, and now, with a little distance, she could see that he had restrained himself and controlled the anger. Not once had he touched Miss Leven, only thumping his fist into the wall in frustration once the nursemaid had left.

Her reaction had been visceral and uncontrollable. Richard's outburst of anger had transported her back to the house she had shared with her husband. She'd imagined fingers closing round her neck, a hand meeting her face or a fist in her belly.

Of course, her reaction was grossly unfair. Richard had never hurt her and she knew he never would.

He was the complete opposite of Phillip. He was kind and considerate and she'd never seen him angry before.

Yet when he had shown real distress, coming out as anger rather than tears or shock, she had pushed him away, fled from Farnleigh Hall without once considering his feelings.

'All this time he has supported you, and the first time he has shown a hint of needing you, you weren't there,' she muttered to herself.

Then she had fled all the way to Bamburgh. At the time it had felt like the only solution, but now she realised what a gulf it had put between them. It hurt to think how Richard must be feeling and she wished she had never abandoned him.

Before they left, she sat at the little table in the corner of the room and wrote a brief note to Richard. She didn't know if he would reply, if he could ever think of forgiving her. Perhaps this time she had pushed him away too hard.

Once she and Noah were ready, they started the walk through Bamburgh to Mrs Wilson's house on the outskirts. She was lucky enough to run into the housekeeper of Farnleigh Hall out shopping for supplies and she passed her the note, asking her to deliver it to Lord Westbridge.

Feeling that she could do no more at present, Hetty

pushed on to Mrs Wilson's house. She hoped the widow would not mind keeping an eye on Noah whilst she worked, but she could not imagine it would be a problem. He would happily sit at the table and draw, or play with the soldiers she had brought along with them.

Mr Brent was in better spirits than she had seen him before and Hetty felt a flicker of hope that he might yet survive his injuries. It would take months of applying careful dressings whilst his skin formed over the wounds, but that would not be the end of the matter. People who had suffered burns found their skin was thickened and tight if it did repair itself, and that could cause any number of problems with function of the limbs. That worry was for another day though. Right now, each hour Mr Brent survived was a miracle and she needed to concentrate on ensuring that infection of his wounds did not occur.

'I have been taking the medicine as you suggested,' he told her. 'Sparingly, but to ease the pain if I need to move. I took a little about half an hour ago to make me groggy for your visit.'

'I am pleased,' Hetty said, setting to work on removing the dressings. The bag of her supplies had been waiting for her at Mrs Wilson's house so she was glad to be able to change the dressings as planned. 'You are looking better.'

'Mrs Wilson feeds us well. Sometimes the portions are more than one man could manage.' He lowered his voice even though they were the only ones in the room. 'I also think my recovery is helped by knowing my wife and my son will be cared for, no matter what. Lord Westbridge is a good man, there are not many as generous as he.'

'He is a good man.'

It took about half an hour to change the dressings and clean any wounds that needed it, and by the end she had a faint sense of hope that Mr Brent would survive his ordeal. It would be many months before they knew for sure, but he had rallied since being moved here to Bamburgh.

Once everything was tidied away, she left the soldier to rest and went downstairs to retrieve Noah. Mrs Wilson had been only too pleased to sit him down with a plate of biscuits and had allowed him to spread his toy soldiers out on the table.

'Mr Brent is improving under your care,' Hetty said as she entered the kitchen. 'Thank you. He tells me your food is delicious and hearty.'

'I think the body needs both food and rest to heal. I can provide him with both,' Mrs Wilson said, beaming.

Hetty looked around, suddenly realising that Noah was not in the kitchen where she had left him.

'Lord Westbridge came by a few minutes ago. Noah was thrilled to see him. The Earl took him outside. I hope I didn't do the wrong thing.'

Forcing a smile on her face, Hetty shook her head. She felt her stomach lurch and her hands begin to tremble. 'No, of course not. I will see where they have got to. I shall return in three days to dress the wounds again.'

'Very good, Mrs Fairweather. I will send for you if anything changes.'

Hetty said a hasty goodbye and hurried out, stopping abruptly on the doorstep as she saw Richard's carriage outside. Noah and Richard were nowhere to be seen, so she assumed they must be in the carriage. With a pounding heart she approached, thanking the coachman as he hopped down to open the door for her.

'Mama!' Noah squealed. 'Richard is here!' He looked happier than he had done since leaving Farnleigh Hall, snuggled up next to Richard, who was showing him some pictures in a brightly illustrated book.

'Hetty,' Richard said, offering her a tentative but genuine smile.

She cleared her throat nervously and wondered if she should climb in.

'I will not bite, and I am not here to abduct you,'

Richard said, holding out a hand to help her up. 'I wish to spend a little time with Noah and we have much to discuss.'

He seemed calm, but underneath the façade she could see the tension in his jaw and in the way he gripped the pages of the book he was holding.

'Very well,' she said, taking a seat opposite Richard and Noah.

Her son and his father practically ignored her the whole journey back to Farnleigh Hall, not through malice but because they were both so engrossed in the book Richard had brought with him. It was an illustrated guide to all the animals in the world and Noah was fascinated by the pictures of the exotic creatures, animals he had not known even existed until a few minutes ago.

'I want crocodile,' he said, stabbing a pudgy finger at the picture in the book.

'A crocodile would eat you for breakfast and come back for Sooty for lunch,' Richard said, his voice just jovial enough to stop Noah from being scared by the idea.

'No crocodile,' Noah said firmly.

'Good decision,' Richard murmured before they moved on to elephants and hippopotamuses.

Before long, the carriage turned into the grounds of Farnleigh Hall and started up the drive. When it rolled to a stop Richard hopped out and helped first Noah and then Hetty down. His fingers lingered for just a moment on hers and Hetty felt a rush of emotion. She had missed him terribly and now she was back where he had made her feel safe, the first place she had felt at home in a long time, but she did not know if she had ruined everything with her reaction to him the day before.

'Let me get Noah settled. Don't go anywhere,' Richard said.

It was Whitely, Richard's trusted footman, who came out to play with Noah, bringing Sooty with him. For a moment Hetty watched the excitable puppy jump up at Noah and she revelled in her son's giggles of delight as the dog licked him exuberantly.

'We will sit where we can see him,' Richard said as he returned to her. She was grateful for his consideration even in this. After the incident in the stables, she preferred to have Noah within her sight, even if she knew he was with someone responsible.

They made their way to a little bench that looked out over the lawn but was far enough from the house that it ensured they had privacy. No one would disturb them here.

Richard remained quiet and Hetty could see he was troubled, as if he didn't know how to start, so she decided to speak first.

'I do not think I will ever be free of Phillip and the fear he beat into me,' she said quietly, jumping right in. 'It is part of me now and as much as I wish to banish it, I doubt I will ever be able to entirely.'

'I would never hurt you, Hetty.'

'I know,' she said. 'As I sit here I know that. Even in the stables the rational part of my mind knew that, but there are times when something takes over me. I cannot predict when it will happen or what will trigger it, but it is all-consuming.' She gave a little smile. 'When I arrived here, even the slightest touch would set it off.'

'But you do not think things will improve further?'

Hetty considered this. 'I expect they will. Our minds have a wonderful ability to suppress things. But just as the images of your comrades lying slaughtered on the battlefield will never leave you, I do not think this will ever be gone completely. I hope one day I will wake up and realise it has been years since I felt overwhelmed by fear and panic, but I acknowledge it is not something within my control.'

It was cathartic just saying the words. For so long she had blamed herself for the panic she felt, as if it was a product of her conscious mind, something she could control. Accepting it was not something she could actively change, that she had to just allow time to work its healing magic, absolved her from some of the guilt she felt for her reactions.

She sighed. 'Yesterday I was ready to say yes to your proposal. I wish I had, that I had refused to take the time to think about it and had given you the answer that was in my heart.'

Richard remained silent. He looked a little broken and Hetty hated that she had done this to him.

'One of my fears is that I will hurt you. That I will not love you as you deserve, because you deserve the very best. More than that, I worry that if we were together these episodes might wear you down. I cannot control them; the panic is overwhelming and sudden and all-encompassing. Imagine being married to me and that was my reaction when you did something you thought innocuous.'

Richard frowned and Hetty was surprised to see there was a flash of anger in his eyes. 'Do you think me a man of little substance, Hetty? Of weak character? Unable to survive a little adversity?'

'No,' she said, placing a placating hand on his leg. 'You are one of the bravest, most resilient people I have ever met.' She smiled sadly. 'But you have suffered. You have lost your entire family and witnessed killing on a grand scale in the war. You deserve an easy life now.' She took a shuddering breath. 'I also know that I have made this all about me. Your reaction in the stables…it came from a place of fear, a place of darkness.'

Richard nodded, his eyes fixed for a moment on his lap before they came up to meet hers.

'I have moments where I do not feel in control, where panic and darkness overwhelm me, but I would never hurt you in those moments, Hetty.'

'I know,' she said softly. He looked anguished and she hated that she had made him feel that way. 'I want to help you with them, to be a strong, dependable force that you know you can rely on, but I do not know how I will react the next time it happens.' She searched his face for his reaction. 'I fear you deserve more than a woman who flees in fear when you need her support the most.'

He shook his head impatiently. 'You keep telling me what I deserve, but you do not stop to ask what it is I want.'

Hetty chewed on her lip. He was right. She hadn't stopped to ask him what he wanted in all of this. The events of the last twenty-four hours might have made him reconsider his proposal.

'What is it you want, Richard?'

'You. Every single part of you. I want to share the good times and support you in the bad times. For that is what a partner does. I am strong enough to love you even when you push me away.'

'You want me even now? After what I have put you through the last few days?'

'Yes,' he said, holding her eye so she would see he was sincere. 'I cannot promise to always remain completely in control, but I do promise I will never hurt you or Noah, and I wish you did not feel overwhelmed in certain situations, but it would not stop me from loving you.'

'Love...' she murmured.

'Yes, love. I love you, Hetty.'

She nodded, her mouth suddenly dry. 'Do you know what I realised when I was crying into my pillow last night?'

He shook his head.

'I realised I had a very rigid idea of love.' She let out a little laugh and wondered if she sounded hysterical. 'I think it was because when we were in Portugal I felt such an overwhelming love for you that I wanted to shout from the rooftops. There was a hint of mania to it, I suppose. I had never been in love before, never felt loved before. Then there was you, my perfect man, who adored me and who I loved with every ounce of my being.'

There was a momentary smile on Richard's lips

as he remembered the giddy feeling of finding love amongst all the destruction.

'When I saw you again, I didn't feel that instant flash of love, the all-consuming variety that we had in Portugal. I was numbed from the last few years I'd spent with Phillip and worn down with worry. It meant that I thought I could never love again, that I was too damaged by my past.'

Now Richard reached out for her, his hand resting gently on her knee as if he realised how difficult it was for her to articulate her thoughts.

'What I did feel was a deep longing for you, a need to be near you, a sadness when I had not seen you for a few hours. I felt like I wanted to spend all my time just the three of us, with the interference of no one else.'

Understanding dawned in Richard's eyes and with it she saw hope.

'As I was lying in bed feeling terribly sorry for myself, I realised that love doesn't have to be a thunderbolt, it can take other forms. Less showy, less dramatic, but perhaps even stronger because it is flourishing despite all the hardships and all the barriers.' Hetty took a moment to compose herself before continuing. 'What I am building up to is to say that I love you, Richard. I am so sorry I did not realise it sooner, that I did not identify the happiness I felt with you, the comfort and the sense of purpose as love, but that is exactly what it is.'

'You love me?'

'I do.' She smiled. 'Probably more than you love me.'

'Impossible.'

'I have been an absolute fool,' she said quietly. 'I have pushed you away at every opportunity, told you I could never love you. I cannot even begin to imagine how that would feel.'

'I will never tell you I don't love you,' Richard said. 'You have my promise.'

'I know.' She smiled more broadly. 'It is one of the many, many reasons I love you.'

Richard put his hands on her waist and ever so gently pulled her towards him. She did not resist, allowing him to topple her onto his lap.

'We have a problem,' he said as he kissed her neck.

'Oh?'

'I gave you my vow that if you refused my proposal I would accept your answer and not ask again.'

'Ah,' Hetty said and pretended to struggle to get up. 'I suppose I will have to pack my bags after all.'

Richard held her firmly. 'You could become my mistress,' he mused. 'But the gossip would set Northumberland on fire. Perhaps not. I cannot see a way out of this predicament.'

'You could break your vow.'

'I do not break promises.'

Hetty smiled up at him. 'Then there is only one thing for it. Will you marry me, Richard?'

'I thought you would never ask,' he murmured before lowering his lips to hers and kissing her deeply.

Epilogue

1817

There were clouds in the sky above, dark and menacing, and Hetty could only hope that the rain would hold off until the festivities were over. This day had been long in the planning and she wanted everything to run smoothly.

As she lifted her hand to shield her eyes and study the clouds, the rings on her left hand caught the light and glinted. For a moment she paused, reveling in her happiness. There was a band of gold upon her finger with a beautiful emerald set in it, surrounded by diamonds. It was no doubt a beautiful piece, but Hetty loved the plain, simple band of metal that sat below it even more. Richard had told her about his planned proposal in Portugal, where he had nothing but this simple metal band to propose with, and how it was stopped from happening by the attack on the village. She had treasured the plain ring ever since as a symbol of how their love had begun.

Somewhere to her left the band started up, it was a cheerful tune and certainly had a military edge to it.

'Why do I feel like I am about to be ordered to lead a march across Europe?' Richard murmured in her ear as he came up behind her.

'I think the band is a wonderful touch,' Hetty said. 'It reminds people of the point of all this.' She waved her hand vaguely in the direction of Thornley House Hospital. Today was the official opening and she had spent weeks organising the grand event. The celebration today would allow the local people to understand what it was they were going to be doing at Thornley House, as well as giving the investors a chance to look around before the first of the patients arrived.

'Today is a roaring success already,' Richard said, wrapping his arms around her for just a moment and kissing her behind the ear. Although it had been almost a year since they had married, they were still in that wonderful period where Society gave them a little latitude to act foolishly around each other. The odd discreet kiss would be excused. 'And I have seen two new potential donors here in the crowd, which is excellent. I will allow them to hear the speeches and then I will approach them directly.'

Hetty nodded, feeling a roil of nerves at the mention of speeches. She felt confident in dealing with injuries and treating wounds, but standing up in front of all these people would test her. Still, it was a challenge she had volunteered for, knowing her words would be powerful alongside Richard's.

'Two minutes and we will get started,' Richard said as he slipped away, no doubt to ensure some aspect of the afternoon was running seamlessly.

'Hetty!' an excited voice called out and Hetty was pleased to see Rose running through the crowd.

'You must call her Lady Westbridge,' Rose's mum chided as they drew closer.

Rose pulled a face and then brandished a book. 'I have finished it. I stayed up all last night reading. I think it is my favourite book ever.'

Hetty smiled. Since Richard had delivered the first pile of books when Rose had been laid up in bed with her broken leg, something rather magical had occurred. The young girl had delighted in how she could escape into the pages of the stories, helping her fend off the boredom of her convalescence. Even when she was back on her feet she had wanted to continue her reading and Richard and Hetty had happily welcomed her into their library. Every few weeks she would appear on their doorstep, a pile of books under her arm to return. Then she would spend half an hour choosing more to take away with her. The books were always returned in pristine condition and Rose was well on her way to gaining the skills she would need to be a schoolteacher, as was her ambition.

'Then you shall have to come and take tea with me in the drawing room at Farnleigh Hall and tell me all about it,' Hetty said with a smile.

At that moment Richard ascended the steps in front of the doors of Thornley House Hospital and called for everyone's attention. Before he started speaking, Noah darted up onto the steps and slipped his hand into his father's. Hetty felt a rush of love for the two people that meant the world to her and unconsciously her hand drifted to her belly. She was not far enough along in her pregnancy for it to be obvious to the world yet, but she was sure that there was a baby growing inside her. It felt like the last piece of a very perfect puzzle. She had worried about Noah's place if they had a boy, but Richard's solicitor had assured her that the legal paperwork meant that Noah was now viewed as Richard's son and heir.

'Thank you all for coming out here today to support us. In opening Thornley House Hospital here today we hope to change the lives of hundreds of brave men who have served their country and been injured whilst in service. This will be a dedicated space where they can come to recuperate and recover from their wounds, learn to navigate the world with their injuries, and once their physical recovery is well on its way, to learn the skills that will ensure they can find employment and support their families.

'This is only possible due to the generosity of our donors, and I thank you all from the very bottom of my heart for believing in this vision as much as we do.'

He motioned for Hetty to come up and join him and she took her place by his side. Noah slipped his other hand into hers and they stood together, looking out over the assembled guests.

'Today, I want to introduce you to someone very special,' Hetty said, her voice loud and clear, travelling to the very back of the crowd. 'When I first met him, he was unable to move, covered in burns from a terrible fire onboard his ship. I think it is not unfair to say he was waiting to die. Every movement he made was agony and he could not think of a time when he might be back on his feet, able to do so many normal things again.

'It is only a year since I met him, but his strength and determination, alongside good medical care and a nurturing environment, mean that he is able to walk up here today and address you all. I give you Mr Brent.'

The crowd parted as Mr Brent made his way through. He walked with a stick, favouring his right side, but his movements were fluid and his pace fast.

'Thank you, Lord and Lady Westbridge,' Mr Brent said, swallowing as he realised how many people he was addressing today. 'Lady Westbridge is right. Little over a year ago I lay in the bed I could no longer share with my wife, for fear she might accidentally brush against my wounds, waiting for death. I sustained serious burns to my body, my neck, my arm and my leg whilst serving in His Majesty's Navy. I was discharged home with no pension, only a few weeks of pay to sustain myself, my wife and our young child.' He paused and Hetty could see the glint of tears in his eyes.

'Today I can walk, I can work, I can look after my family.' He smiled at his wife and son, who were standing near the front. 'I can embrace my wife, I can pick up my son. A year ago, I did not believe any of that possible, yet I am a testament to what can be done.'

There was thunderous applause from the crowd and Richard allowed it to go on for twenty seconds before he raised a hand for silence.

'It is my honour to say that Mr Brent will be working here at Thornley House Hospital, and alongside his other duties I know he will inspire the soldiers and sailors that come after him.'

Richard held up a key and then passed it to Hetty.

'Are you sure? It is your dream.'

'I'm sure,' he said with a smile, then turned to the crowd. 'Thornley House Hospital is officially open.'

The event lasted for hours and was a huge success, with interest from the local people who would be vital in helping to support the hospital, but also from a few new donors too. As Richard closed the door after the last guest had left he felt a swell of triumph.

He smiled as he saw Noah collapsed on a chair, fast asleep, overcome by the excitement of the day. Then his gaze went to where Hetty was talking to one of the maids, letting her know what was needed to get the hospital ready to receive their first patient in the morning.

'How do you feel?' Richard asked as Hetty finished with the maid and came over to him. She looked tired but happy. He was keen she didn't overexert herself now they knew she was pregnant, but trying to suggest she did less was never going to go down well. He'd stopped insisting she rest and instead focused his efforts on employing a few extra people so Hetty's workload was lightened a little.

Time would tell whether this had been a successful strategy or not, but it was worth a try.

'Tired, but content. I think I will collapse into bed as soon as we get home.'

'You always make the best plans, Lady Westbridge,' he said, raising a suggestive eyebrow.

'Collapse into bed to sleep,' she clarified.

'We all know I will be lying chastely, trying my very hardest to sleep, and it will be your wandering hands that cannot control themselves,' he whispered in her ear.

Hetty laughed and Richard felt a wave of happiness wash over him. Her laugh was his favourite sound in the world, closely followed by Noah's.

She slipped her hand into his and together they made one last tour of the building, ensuring that everything was in place. Only when they had checked each room did they return to where Noah was still sleeping.

'The hospital is open,' Hetty said, rising up on tiptoes and brushing a kiss against his lips. 'You are in the very privileged position of having realised your dream.'

'Today was a success,' Richard agreed.

'And tomorrow the hard work begins.'

'Someone once told me that the greatest reward came from the hardest work. A nurse, I think, someone I met on the Peninsular.' He grinned. 'Have I ever told you how lucky I know I am?'

'Once or twice,' Hetty said with a smile. 'Although a lady is always happy to hear such praise again.'

'I am the luckiest man alive,' he said, bringing her hand up to his lips and kissing the soft skin. 'Do you know my favourite moment ever was the day you and Noah walked back into my life? Everything good I have built from there.'

'I love you,' Hetty said as she narrowed the gap between them for another kiss.

'I love you too.' He kissed her again and then motioned towards Noah. 'Let us get Noah home and in bed, then I will kiss you some more.'

'Is that a promise?'

'It is. And you know I never break a promise.'

* * * * *

*If you enjoyed this story,
make sure to pick up Laura Martin's
The Cinderella Shepherd Sisters miniseries*

One Waltz with the Viscount
One Forbidden Kiss with the Laird

*Why not also check out
Laura Martin's other great reads*

A Housemaid to Redeem Him
The Kiss That Made Her Countess

MILLS & BOON®

Coming next month

DARING TO DREAM OF THE DUKE
Lauri Robinson

Book 1 in Brides for Sworn Bachelors

There was something in Michael's eyes, the way he was looking at her, that was stealing the air from her lungs. Making it hard to breathe and impossible to look away. It felt as if time stopped. As if the world forgot to keep turning.

She had the strangest sensation that he wanted to kiss her. Or maybe those were her thoughts. For that was exactly what she wanted. With every part of her body.

His finger was still beneath her chin, and his thumb was caressing her cheek and sending a thrilling heat through her face, down her neck. Her lips were tingling, her heart was pounding, and the rest of her had the greatest desire to rise on her toes so her face was closer to his.

She'd never wanted something so badly. So completely. An unusual excitement was growing stronger and stronger at the mere idea of kissing him. Of his lips touching hers. She could imagine that it would be better than dancing with him. Better than anything she'd ever known.

Just as she was giving in, about to rise onto her toes, a piercing sense of reality struck. This was Michael. The one man she'd always dreamed of kissing and the one man she couldn't kiss. Couldn't ever let him know about the dreams she'd had for years. He'd merely been being kind to her this weekend, watching out for her, because as Nora had mentioned that first day, he thought of her as another sister. Someone he had to protect. Nora had said that would never change, and he certainly hadn't done anything to make Rosemary believe otherwise.

She'd been the one wishing it would change, and she shouldn't have. It wouldn't matter what she wore—he would never see her as a woman he could be interested in for something more than friendship.

Coming to her senses, she jerked her head backwards, and knowing that wasn't enough, she took a step backwards, too, all the while struggling to catch her breath.

The hand that had been touching her face fell to Michael's side, and it suddenly felt like she'd lost something precious.

He stared at her for yet another stilled moment, and she wished with all her might that she could read his mind. She couldn't, so all she could do was hope that he hadn't realized how badly she'd wanted him to kiss her.

Continue reading

DARING TO DREAM OF THE DUKE
Lauri Robinson

Available next month
millsandboon.co.uk

Copyright © 2026 Lauri Robinson

COMING SOON!

We really hope you enjoyed reading this book. If you're looking for more romance be sure to head to the shops when new books are available on

Thursday 26th March

To see which titles are coming soon, please visit
millsandboon.co.uk/nextmonth

MILLS & BOON

FOUR BRAND NEW BOOKS FROM
MILLS & BOON MODERN

Indulge in desire, drama, and breathtaking romance – where passion knows no bounds!

OUT NOW

Eight Modern stories published every month, find them all at:

millsandboon.co.uk

LET'S TALK
Romance

For exclusive extracts, competitions and special offers, find us online:

- **f** MillsandBoon
- **X** @MillsandBoon
- **📷** @MillsandBoonUK
- **♪** @MillsandBoonUK

Get in touch on 01413 063 232

For all the latest titles coming soon, visit
millsandboon.co.uk/nextmonth